Bitter Apples

Cursed Morsels Press

Contents

Foreword

I worked as a high school English teacher for six years before leaving the profession. I still miss teaching, and even more than that, I miss my students—especially the morbid, hilarious Horror Lit kids.

Sometimes I consider returning, only to remember the many unpleasant parts of the job. Small irritations like students watching anime on their phones during class discussions and administrators calling hour-long meetings that could have been emails.

But there were much worse aspects of teaching, too—ugly, frightening aspects. Students stressed to the point of suicidal ideation. Teachers not making enough money to cover their medical bills. School board members hellbent on making life miserable for queer students.

These examples barely scratch the surface of the horrors I encountered in the profession. I'm relieved to be in a different job, but I often think about my former coworkers and students who are still there. What new fear, stress, and trauma are they going through? And how much can they endure before they break?

With these anxious questions in mind, I decided to put together *Bitter Apples*, a horror anthology that examines the dark side of teaching. Every writer featured in this book has worked as a teacher.

Their stories reflect a unique and often personal perspective on teacher terrors. While this anthology is fiction, it goes to some frighteningly real places. A list of content warnings can be found in the back of the book.

As one last note, I'd like to dedicate this book to my parents, both of whom survived the true horrors of teaching. Love you, Mom and Dad.

Eric Raglin

Editor-in-chief of Cursed Morsels Press

There's a Reason They Collect the Pencils

Corey Farrenkopf

T he mental hospital wasn't abandoned, but Clive knew it would happen some day. All asylums fall to the same fate. The chipped tile. The forgotten wheelchairs and tattered yellow curtains, some teenagers having snuck in to spray paint *Satan Rains* on the padded room walls, ghosts moaning down every hall. But that's years off. Today, Clive runs a K-5 History class followed by a 6-12 English class on the ART floor. Tomorrow they'll move on to Math and Science.

Clive doesn't think it's right to force a kid who recently attempted suicide to do Trigonometry, but the state says otherwise.

He really needs the job, despite the philosophical disagreement.

Despite the ghosts.

"We're going over sonnets today," he says, standing at the front of a ring of desks, a whiteboard at his back, Shakespeare's Sonnet 18 diagrammed over his shoulder. The classroom, like every room in the hospital, hangs heavy with antiseptic scents and the glare of fluorescent lighting. The students sit in a half-circle of rounded desks, tapping pre-counted pencils as six orderlies watch from various corners of the room, waiting for someone to lose their cool and require restraint. Clive hopes today isn't one of those days. It's hard to get used to a three-hundred-pound bodybuilder type pinning a hundred-pound thirteen-year-old to the chipped linoleum floor. But there is a reason they collect the pencils at the end of the two hours.

No one responds meaningfully to Clive's introduction. A few students groan, but some like the rhymes. Others hate the meter. Most don't care one way or the other.

"Hey, it's going to be fun. Write something funny, or something serious, or whatever. Poetry is off the wall. Half the good ones sound like prayers to ancient gods or something otherworldly."

Some of the students perk up. An orderly in the back coughs, tattooed arms crossed across his bench-pressed chest, giving Clive the eye. Clive knows he's supposed to keep lessons grounded, that the kids need the tangible rather than the abstract, but how are you supposed to teach poetry that way? Everything about it is vague interpretations and hymns to the dead.

"Or you could write about a favorite pet. Or a friend. Or a tree. Who doesn't love a good tree poem?"

Clive writes an example on the board about his cat allergies, detailing rhyming patterns and length, *sneeze* complimenting *wheeze*. The kids follow along half stoned from the mix of prescriptions and the lack of sleep from neighboring residents howling at night. No one laughs at Clive's cat jokes.

"Can I write one about my mom?" A thin blonde boy named Sal asks.

"You can write about whatever you want. Whatever moves you," Clive replies.

Sal rarely speaks. For him to show interest at all is a win. Long before his suicide attempt, Sal lived in an Eastern European orphanage where he was confined to a crib, swaddled almost every hour of the day, resulting in extreme detachment.

Sal nods, but doesn't pick up his pencil, doesn't even look at his paper.

The second Sal is already on his second rhyming couplet.

The translucent ghost twin sits just next to the boy, in the same spot he occupies every day. Clive can clearly see the shimmering lines of his face crease in concentration as he jots words onto ethereal paper. Every students' double does the same, a newsroom full of ghosts scribbling away at the assignment, seated at spectral desks mirroring the true arrangement, one for each student.

While the decrepitude of the asylum is years off, the ghosts are already there. Clive sees them every day, trailing his students into the classroom, shadows of alternate selves, who they could have been if they weren't exposed to gratuitous amounts of lead in infancy, or if Uncle Roger hadn't done what he had done on that family trip, or if … the list goes on. Plenty of students like Sal had chemical imbalances, some lever accidentally switched in their brains. Their ghosts are there too, not wearing the constant pajama apparel of the ART floor, but something more fitting for church, collars and ties and dresses draping below the knee. The living students wear socks with grippies on the bottom, the crust of sleep always in their eyes, T-shirts with cartoon characters covering their chests.

"No rush, guys. Take as much time as you need," Clive says. The room is still. No one writes. It's like this everyday. Lesson plans dissolving into silence. Most eyes track the sparrows outside the windows, or scan the outdated chapter books lining the bookshelves in the back of the room.

Only the ghosts are writing, enjoying the process of putting thoughts into words, getting some time out of their own heads.

At least someone's getting something out of this, Clive thinks, sitting down at his own desk, turning on his phone timer.

A fifteen-minute free write is a fifteen-minute free write.

———— ◆ ————

Clive had asked the orderlies if they could see the second children during his first month on the floor. Each looked at him like he was the one who should be committed and given a room on the fifth floor with the geriatric patients. No one saw the other lives the children lived, those ethereal figures hovering at their heels, always attempting to nudge their present selves into something better. Only Clive can see their efforts. It does no good mentioning it to anyone else. He often doubts anything is going to help the kids. His lesson on state capitals certainly isn't rewriting years of trauma.

———— ◆ ————

The K-5 class has fewer kids in it than the 6-12. The ART floor is in the process of shutting down. No new students are given beds, no new intake forms fill Clive's inbox. The hospital is starting a second methadone unit in place of the children's ward. Such moves are common across the state. There's more money in adult care than in children's, so out the beds go, the few hospitals left with such floors racking up wait lists of impossible lengths. Clive knows he has three months of employment left, tops. He's been job hunting, but the prospects are bleak.

Today only eight students sit before Clive.

On the board he draws an elaborate maze, marking every few spaces with a line-drawn monster, a fraction hovering above its head. It's his improvised Dungeons and Dragons class meant to teach probability and percentages. Some of the kids love it. Some hate it. But like most things, they are generally indifferent to it.

Lynn is one of the few who loves it.

At least on her good days.

Lynn is seven, very short, with fiery red hair, and a blood-lead level five times higher than what the human body can usually handle. Some days she can focus and remember Clive's name. Others, she drops on all fours and attempts to bite her classmates, all connection to the present severed. The pattern is always the same. Lynn's double barely looks up from her work as her near-sister sinks incisors into the sleeve of an orderly before he drags her away to a padded room.

"I want to fight the dragon," Lynn says when her turn comes.

The dragon has a one-in-six chance of being conquered. Clive knows Lynn doesn't understand how improbable that is, but he won't smother her excitement. Instead, he hands her the die.

"Give it a roll," he says.

Lynn smiles and shakes the white cube in her fist before dropping it on the desk. The die makes a sharp clicking sound before it tumbles to a six.

"No way, you got the dragon," Clive says, almost reaching out for a high five, before catching himself. Sudden movements are a no go. Bodily contact with students is also against the rules, so Clive moves to the board and draws a little stick figure Lynn on the other side of the dragon, ready to face whatever the labyrinth brings next.

Her ghost gives a little fist bump to the empty air and smiles at Clive.

He smiles back.

One of the orderlies looks at him, head cocked, before Clive readjusts himself. He pretends to sneeze. It's his usual cover-up. No one normally smiles at Lynn. The purple rictus-shaped bruises up and down the orderly's arms explain why.

The lead was in the pipes of her childhood home. And the paint on the walls. No one knows how she is still alive, but there she sits before him for two hours every day, occasionally slaying dragons, occasionally believing she is the dragon.

"Now who wants to take on the minotaur?" Clive asks.

Three hands shoot up.

Maybe they'll just play D&D everyday until they shut down the ward. That wouldn't be so bad.

———◦———

"You can always go back to doing carpentry with your dad," Violet says, as they walk over the old train bridge spanning the Connecticut River. They trace the same path each day after work, attempting to destress from their jobs.

"You know he doesn't want me to do that," Clive replies. "He always wanted me to work with my head, not my body, and I get that on some level. Think about his back problems, and his shoulder, and his ACL, and—"

"Hey, I get it," Violet says, nudging Clive with her elbow. "I'm just saying you have a fallback if we ever get screwed for rent."

"Yeah, I guess I could put in a few months and he wouldn't mind. Be a nice little bit of father-son bonding time."

The water beneath their feet is smooth and dark green. Lush foliage creeps along the bankings just above the line of mud that makes up the Connecticut's shore. Clive traces the current with his eyes, focusing on the ducks paddling in the shallows, chewing weeds. Life should be that simple, he thinks, gazing at his smudged reflection in the water below, ghostlike in metaphor only, too similar to that second self haunting the ART floor. He avoids mirrors at work, that shimmer out of the corner of his eye, dodging a more literal spectral interpretation.

"Did she do it again today?" Violet asks, pulling Clive from his reverie.

Clive nods. "It's the third time this week. They said they might not let Lynn go to class anymore if she keeps it up. Supposedly there's some clause in the law that allows education to be withheld under certain circumstances."

"Maybe it's for her own good. How many people has she bitten? Five? Ten?"

"I don't keep track."

Lynn had attacked one of her classmates that morning, biting their thigh, teeth slicing through flannel. The orderlies tranquilized her on the spot. When the needle went in, Lynn's body fell limp, all crazed anger washed from her face, replaced with an innocent calm. Only the blood at the corner of her mouth told a different story.

"But she needs to stay in class. It makes her happy, sometimes. It's possibly the only time she gets a chance to do something fun," Clive says. "We've only got one month left. She deserves that at least."

"Just don't get too close, right? I don't want you coming home all bandaged up or worse."

"I know, I know. Trust me, I'm well aware of the distance required."

———◦○◦———

The ghost students are playing together at the back of the room. Looping hand in hand, they form a human chain winding around

Ray, the largest of the orderlies, singing a song Clive can't hear. Their lips move, but no vocalization escapes. Their more solid counterparts are pushing glass beads around on their desk as Clive attempts to teach them simple shortcuts for multiplication.

It isn't as exciting as percentage-based D&D, but life skills are important too.

The ghosts of the orderlies are there as well, leaning against the far wall, slightly better dressed than their concrete counterparts, thinner or more muscular or with a better hairline, just shaking their heads as translucent children loop another lap.

Lynn sits in the desk closest to the front. She appears more asleep than awake. The meds the clinicians moved her to are much stronger than her previous dose. She didn't even perk up when Clive mentioned the return of their dragon hunt tomorrow. Her eyes are closed, her breath almost undetectable. Clive asked Ray to check on her once to make sure she hadn't crossed over to the world of the students dancing at the back of the class, but she stirred and gave a little chuckle.

Clive moves his own glass beads around his desk to show students how to multiply, placing two here, then four there, then eight. The line of ghost children breaks formation and washes over to their counterparts, fingers falling to the beads they can't touch. Clive knows that if they could, they'd get every question right. Multiplication would be one of the simplest steps in their lives.

"Now's your turn," Clive says, scribbling four different problems on the board. "It's all you."

A few of the students move the beads around, the sound of glass clinking against glass pinging through the room with each problem solved.

Ray waves for Clive to join him at the back, nothing subtle about the gesture.

"They tell you it's all over next week?" he asks as Clive reaches his side, not quiet enough to go unnoticed by their students. They stir, the less sedate ones turning an ear to their conversation. "Funding's run dry faster than they thought it would."

"What are they doing with the kids?" Clive asks, tone hushed, hoping Ray will get the hint.

"Ship them off to another hospital or just discharge them if they're close enough to their end date."

"But I thought all the nearby hospitals were full."

"Oh, they are. They'll just put the kids up on some non-psych floor until things open. It's messed up. They're going to lose all their progress. Guarantee you everyone will backslide and forget the coping skills they've been working on."

The ghost Ray nods along with every word.

"Is there something we can do about that? Some way to help?"

"Nada, my friend. The admins aren't going to care where they go as long as the insurance money keeps coming in. Doesn't matter where the bed is, just as long as someone's in it."

The ghosts have left their desks and are back to looping around Ray, this time incorporating Clive into their widening circle, lips moving, their silent song flung to unseen ears. Clive thought he'd have more time, more days to straighten his life out, more days to help his students in whichever way he could. But what had he really done for them? He asked himself the same question every week. Every day.

He wasn't wiping suicidal ideation from their minds by playing word games, wasn't soothing the swelling rage of ODD with his complimentary colors lessons. When he first started the job, Clive thought he could make a difference, but the system just chugged on, pushing the kids along until they were out the door, free for a day or so before they were brought back or shipped off to another hospital, one in which they hadn't overstayed their welcome. Nothing was eased. Nothing erased.

Clive catches a silver, man-shaped flicker out of the corner of his eye. He knows what his second self is trying to do. Clive is quite familiar with the comforting teacher act, but that isn't what he wants. He needs to get back to the lesson. Distraction won't help the kids.

Does anyone ever get to feel a sense of ease though, Clive wonders as the translucent children skip about his body while he makes his way to the whiteboard.

Does it ever stop for anyone?

———◦○◦———

Sal hands Clive the poem about his mother before he takes the elevator down to the lobby for his release. Clive thought Sal had written about his adopted mother, the woman waiting for him by her SUV in front of the automated hospital doors, but the poem is about his birth mother, the woman he's never known.

It's not sad like Clive expected. Just curious. Twelve lines of wonder about her face, her hands, the sound of her voice when she sings, the way she'd say his name if they crossed paths at the Holyoke Mall. He even makes a joke about cold Romanian winters. *How much snow must the two of us now go (through)*. It's the only line that missed the rhyme scheme.

Sal had been listening after all.

Once the poem is in Clive's hand, Sal steps away without saying anything else. He moves towards the elevator doors. They open for him, they swallow him.

Clive wonders what the translucent Sal might have written, whether he'd even know the true meaning of cold.

The ghosts never follow Clive home. He doesn't know if they actually leave the hospital grounds or if they just vanish at the threshold. The world would be swimming with them otherwise, all those alternative selves birthed from bad decisions, unfortunate genetics, and the thoughtless actions of others. He doesn't want to know what Violet's ghost would look like, how she'd react to his jokes and romantic advances. Even if she could get clearance to meet him at work, he'd never let her on the ART floor. He's happy with the flesh and blood woman before him, not the ideal version that wanders the streets of some other reality.

"How'd the Chipotle interview go?" she asks from the couch, putting down the Playstation controller, some fantasy epic paused on the screen.

"They weren't actually hiring a manager like the advertisement said," Clive replies, loosening his tie. He had to dip out of work early to make the interview and hadn't had time to change. Was a shirt and tie the right decision for a burrito wrapping interview. Clive didn't know, but that's what he went with. "The guy said it's a manager track position. Like I'd start out on the line then move my way up over three years. Starting pays actually thirteen an hour."

"That ad was a bit misleading."

"I think it's what they tell everyone," Clive replies, dropping down on the couch next to Violet, a hand worming across his scalp as he lets out a deep sigh. "I can't believe none of the other teaching jobs got back to me."

"You'd think with a master's they'd be all over you."

"I think everyone in the valley has a master's. Just half of them are taller than me and seem a little better in the disciplinarian department."

That's why Clive always assumed he'd been hired for the hospital job. His calm demeanor. Quiet voice. Unimposing stature. Public schools wanted a guy who used to play football and is cool with coaching JV, not another creative type to fight over who runs the school's singular writing elective.

"Hey, we've got time," Violet said, reaching for his hand, easing his fingers from the roots of his hair, cradling them in her lap. "And worse comes to worse, you wrap burritos for a few months. I bet you'll get a sick discount and we won't have to cook anymore."

Clive laughs.

"They give you free guacamole. It's a pretty steep benefit."

————◦————

Most of the beds on ART are empty. Three students remain in the K-5 wing. Two in 6-12. Classes feel even more eerie than usual. Ghosts are one thing, the empty desks and utter stillness another. Clive can see the hospital's future approaching at a rapid clip, those abandoned halls and spray-painted walls not so far away. The methadone money will be there for a while, then it too will dry up, and mental hospitals will be a thing of the past, just hollowed out structures for pigeons to roost in and ghosts to haunt.

As the students' numbers drop, so do the number of orderlies. The ratio was always one orderly for two students. Now it's just Ray and Selma and their alternative selves. Each pair joins a student for Clive's final class, lowering themselves into the cramped seats next to Hector and Joan, helping them make the right decisions to get through Clive's last percentage-based labyrinth. Their ghosts aid the students' ghosts through their own undead mazes, smiling and laughing with each silent dice roll. Clive takes the seat next to Lynn, who is more awake now than the day before. Her ghost sits across from them, elbows propped on the desk, chin resting in palms, eyes tracing the path before her.

Clive asked his supervisor where Lynn was going once the floor emptied. *Some hospital in Boston. At least while she waits for the right bed.* Clive didn't like to think about what that would look like. He'd heard stories of kids belted to gurneys, doped to the gills because staff wasn't trained to work with psych patients. It wasn't the nurses fault. There are only so many fields you can specialize in.

"You want to tackle the hydra?" Clive asks.

"Hydra?" Lynn says, squinting at the whiteboard Clive places on her desk. The drawing is terrible. The creature is little more than a body with five squiggles blossoming from its neck. Lynn's ghost leans back, forming both of her hands into snake heads, fingers snapping like playful jaws about her face. The creature has a two-in-six chance of being passed.

Clive points to the number written above its head. "It's a little bit easier than the dragon. Think of him as the dragon's younger, less muscular cousin."

"Oh, I can do that," Lynn says, casting the die.

It lands on a three.

Clive shakes his head. "How about we give it another go?"

"Another go," Lynn repeats, picking up the die and rerolling.

It lands on a four, just one shy of the desired outcome. Lynn looks at the number, then up at Clive. Her forehead scrunches. He knows she understands the numbers, that something he's said over the past month has sunk in, even if the answer is disappointing. Her hand starts to shake, clenching and unclenching as her doppelgänger reaches across the table to comfort her, stroking her arm though Lynn can't feel the gesture.

"Hey hey hey. We've got a few more minutes. Give it another roll," Clive says.

"What if I don't get it today?" Lynn asks.

"You will."

"But what about when class is over?"

"Well—"

Clive doesn't know what to say. He doesn't want to lie, to tell her he'll let her try again tomorrow. Tomorrow she'll be on her way to Boston and he'll be unemployed. He'll never see her again. What harm would a lie do? He wouldn't have to deal with the repercussions, the tears and the wailing.

"Maybe they'll be able to play the game with you at the new hos—"

Before Clive can get the words out, Lynn's teeth are bared, fingers scrabbling at the white board, digging furrows into the smooth surface. Clive falls backward out of his chair as she lunges, teeth snapping at his neck. Before Lynn reaches Clive, Ray falls on her, pressing her limbs to the floor in a five-point hold. His bulk stops her in her tracks, but her head still lashes about, trying to bite anything within reach. Her eyes aren't the calm pools they'd been moments before. They are wide, seeing beyond Clive and the classroom and the hospital itself. Can she see her twin, Clive wonders as he scrambles back on hands and knees. Does she know what she's been cheated of?

Her ghost kneels next to her, tears streaming, hand trying to pet the other girl's hair, trying to rub comfort into her scalp. Clive has never seen the ghosts cry before. He's seen them sing and dance and go blissfully on while their counterparts crumple and turn to rage, but not this. Something is different. Maybe ghost Lynn understands the finality of it, that the forking path is beginning to look like a straight road no one wants to be stuck on. The ghost's mouth moves with words Clive can't hear, but he understands nonetheless.

She didn't mean to. She didn't mean to. This isn't what she wants.

"I know it's not. I promise," Clive says as the other orderly, Selma, uncaps a syringe, jabbing the tranquilizer into Lynn's thigh. She falls still, limbs going limp.

"You promise what?" Ray asks, leaning his weight off the girl.

"Nothing," he stammers.

"I knew we shouldn't have been letting you get that close," Ray says. "It was almost a nice send off, you know?"

"Almost," Clive replies.

———— ❦ ————

When Clive leaves at the end of the day, he pauses before he unlocks the door of his old Volvo. He looks up to the fourth floor, to where his past classroom looms over the surrounding highways and the weed-choked runoff pond just beyond the nearest exit. In the window, a pale image of himself presses against the glass, one hand raised to the sun's glare, the other resting on the head of a small girl. They both wave as Clive slips into the driver's seat. He can't bring himself to look back. He doesn't want to see what the right version of himself looks like, what he could have been if things had played out differently and he'd actually been able to help.

It was just a job, he tells himself, pulling out of the spot.

He catches a final glimpse of the glow coming from the upper windows in his mirror, the slow arc of their hands waving back and forth.

At least someone's staying with her, Clive thinks.

He promised himself he'd never bring the ghosts home. Some things have to be forgotten if they can be forgotten. He's just glad he had the choice.

Drip Drop

Emma E. Murray

Z oe was the first and only student I'd ever lost. Seven years old, her whole life ahead of her, and then she was gone. I went to the funeral, touched the closed casket while whispering a goodbye, and cried every night for three weeks. Then she came back.

I was on the couch, cutting shapes for next week's geometry puzzles, when the lights flickered violently before snapping off with the sizzle of fried wires. It shook me up, but other than nearly snipping my fingertips off with the scissors, I didn't think much of it. Just a black-out or maybe an electrical problem. These apartments weren't exactly luxury-grade after all. But when I saw the swirl of gray appear in the kitchen, float over the bar counter toward me, my stomach dropped. I froze. Even before she took form, gossamer-thin and muted, I knew it was Zoe. Before her voice uttered my name, soft and timid, just like in life, every cell in my body ached with the knowledge it couldn't be anything, or anyone, other than her.

"Ms. Wright? Is that you, Ms. Wright?" she asked, shuffling her tiny, incorporeal feet across the carpet. Each footfall was a wet squelch under immaterial weight and left a damp impression that would last for hours, slowly drying in the tepid air. Her hair was loose, thick tendrils dripping with every movement, as if she'd just emerged from some unseen body of water.

"Yes, it's me. Why are you here?" My voice trembled, thick with fresh tears even though I thought I'd cried myself to a numb husk over those weeks since her death.

"I—I don't know. I'm scared. Really scared," she answered, and all I wanted was to hold her. I ran to the girl who'd spent five days of every week with me since August. Perfect attendance. A quiet girl, so young yet already jaded to the world, but I'd worked hard to pull her out of her shell, to show her school could be fun and adults could be kind.

I knew she came from a rough home, but she was always dressed well, hair combed and braided in twin plaits, or sometimes just one long braid of deepest brown down her back, nearly to her waist. The girl who entered my classroom on the first day of school with sullen eyes and a tight jaw, following directions without complaint nor joy, no childhood wonder. The girl whose parents never stopped by, even after I left the message inviting them to a special morning assembly. Zoe was chosen to sing a solo in front of the whole school. They never showed. Not then, not at any conference, not to pick her up or drop her off. Her home life was something foreign and private, beyond my reach.

I ran to the girl and tried to embrace her, but my arms went right through her shimmering body, leaving me shivering cold and dripping wet, the hairs raised on goosepimple flesh. She looked me square in the eye, crouched and hardened, her face distorting from the child I knew into something rotten, flesh hanging in flaps from her cheeks, lips pulled back in a skeletal sneer.

"Why didn't you help me, Ms. Wright? You knew. You had to have known."

I gagged on the sob filling my throat and then the girl softly imploded, millions of particles scampering like cockroaches into herself until she was nothing but an orb of gray light again. In a moment, even that went dim before snuffing itself out. I was alone in my apartment, shaking and rocking on my hands and knees, forehead to the sopping patch of carpet where Zoe had stood.

I was a mess for the next few days at school, but I kept it together as much as I could for the kids. They were mourning and lost too, but it was incredibly hard. I found myself trailing off into silence while giving directions or reading aloud; one of the children always brought me back with a gentle nudge or question. I even started to believe I'd hallucinated the ordeal from some sense of guilt.

But then, exactly one week later, she came to me again.

No misty shape or orb of light appeared this time. Zoe walked out of my bedroom, looking just like her normal self, except dripping wet. I dropped the pile of stories I was scoring, papers fluttering to the carpet. She trampled right over them, translucent wet footprints soaking through, as she stormed towards me.

"You knew! You knew! You knew!" she shouted, her arm arrow-straight, finger aimed at my face. Her lip rose, quivering with a snarl, and I crumpled in on myself.

"Zoe! What are you talking about?" I clawed at my mouth with nervous fingers, pried the words from my parched throat. She stopped just before her finger touched me, less than an inch from my wide-open eye. Then her hand dropped to her side. Disgust melted into a deluge of tears.

"You knew, but you pretended like you didn't. Why didn't you ever ask me? Why didn't you stop him before—before—" She cut herself off with a wail.

I shook my head. I didn't understand, but the wail grew, breaking into multiple voices, all different octaves, the highest like a screaming kettle and the lowest, an ursine rumble. I covered my ears, but the sound cut cleanly through both flesh and bone. Louder and louder, every inch of my apartment filled with unbearable noise, every nerve in my body on the verge of bursting. Her shriek filled me. I swallowed it down, and just when my lungs threatened to give out, suffocated with solid sound, her mouth snapped shut.

The tiny girl turned and walked back into my bedroom, but she didn't disappear. She waited in silence for me all night. At first, I wouldn't enter, but something told me she wouldn't hurt me. I had cared about her, read with her every day. She'd loved nonfiction about animals, especially horses. I'd always loved all my students, not quite the same as a mother's love but still strong, still willing to take a bullet for any of them. Zoe had my heart as much as any other student.

I teared up remembering that, less than a month before, she'd fallen from the monkey bars and I'd sat with her the rest of recess. I let her tell me all about the movie she'd seen over the weekend, one about a little girl and her horse. She had wanted her mother to watch it with her, but she was too busy. Instead, she'd given her a big bag of microwaved popcorn. I'd imagined her alone on her couch, wishing she were the girl in the movie.

At first, I watched her in the dark. Then I beckoned to her, but she didn't speak, didn't move. Eventually, I must have drifted to sleep, but it was fitful, and her eyes burned into me through my dreams. In the morning, she was gone.

Things deteriorated rapidly after that second visit. I constantly caught myself staring at her desk, the name tag removed but bits of tape outlining where it had been. Sometimes I'd realize I was crying, not just a little sniffle but my eyes leaking sieves. At one point, I'd soaked my silk blouse so badly I had to change into a ratty T-shirt I kept in my bag. It was mortifying, but the children didn't tease me. If anything, they were afraid of me.

They'd lost their friend and classmate, and now they'd lost the sunny teacher who'd sing the days of the week, lead them in yoga brain breaks, and always had a Fun Friday craft project waiting, like the tissue paper suncatchers taped across the windows. That teacher was gone, and a stranger who shuffled around, losing her place in books and the simplest math equations, sobbing at her desk during silent reading time, had replaced the one they'd loved. They stopped asking for band-aids and hugs when they skinned their knees at recess, instead toughing it out or seeking one of the other first-grade teachers. They watched me with rabbit eyes and skittish feet. I was worse than the missing friend because I haunted them in person, five days a week.

All I could think of was what Zoe had said, or what I had hallucinated her saying to me. What had I missed? As soon as I let myself delve below the soup-skin thin layer of denial, the signs were all waiting for me, blaring red, a cacophony of sirens drowning out the world.

I *had* seen bruises on her arms, dots of black and purple, lining up perfectly with an adult's grasp, but she hadn't mentioned them, and I hadn't asked for details. The complete lack of contact with her parents, the lunch box nearly empty, childish meals she'd hastily thrown together herself. I'd told myself maybe her mom was busy that morning, maybe she had a younger sibling, a baby who had bawled all night and her parents couldn't think straight enough to pack more than a pudding without a spoon. I hadn't asked and she hadn't complained.

She always seemed wary, afraid even, of all adults, only warming to me after I proved I didn't yell, didn't break her down, didn't shrink her to a nothingness meant to be seen and not heard. I let her opt out of sharing with the whole class, but gently pulled thoughts and opinions from her when we discussed her reading assignments. As she learned I didn't raise my voice, didn't force her to talk, she opened up. Little by little, she smiled more, explained her drawings to me in whispers at the back table, and sometimes even timidly raised her hand, offering a soft answer to be shared with her classmates. But there were still other warning signs. The time she'd wet herself when I wasn't there, the substitute relaying she'd seemed too afraid to approach him, and how her soiled clothing stayed in her backpack, wrapped in a plastic bag, for three weeks before finally going home and staying there.

I pored over every detail I'd noticed and yet hadn't. An intense self-loathing throbbed inside me like a cancer, but still I replayed these details every second of the day until I made myself ill.

Then came the day my principal came in during my lunch and slipped a packet onto my desk about the therapy services covered by our insurance. She awkwardly placed her hand on my shoulder and tiptoed through a rambling speech about being there for the kids. I knew that she was right. I had to do better. They deserved better.

I forced myself to stay late, planning for small groups, crafting interventions for the kids who couldn't solve the math exit ticket, and most importantly, putting together a read aloud and questions to facilitate an age-appropriate conversation about loss. When I finally got home, felt prepared for the first time in weeks, and even a little happier. But then, as I sat on the couch with my microwaved macaroni and trash TV, Zoe appeared next to me, her small, wet body leaving a puddle but not an indent in the cushion.

"Ms. Wright?" Zoe asked. Her pallid face turned to me and rotted away before my eyes, chunks of meat falling with each syllable. But I wasn't afraid.

"I'm so sorry. You were right. I should've said something." I took a deep breath, then asked the question I didn't want to ask. "It wasn't an accident, was it? What happened?"

"He says I slipped in the bath. Mom says she'd been watching me but then walked away for just a few minutes, thinking I was old enough to bathe on my own, but when she came back, it was already too late. They're liars. I wasn't hungry that night. Asked if I could skip dinner, and when he said no, I pushed my food around my plate. That was all. I just wasn't hungry." Sobs interrupted her story and the lights flickered to the meter of her whimpers. She composed herself, forced her story to continue. "He came in when I was in the tub. Held me down and I drowned looking up at his swollen, stupid, red face. I hate him!"

The lightbulbs pulsed to a new level of brightness when she shouted but then hummed back to normal. I reached out to Zoe, trying to comfort her, but again I fell through her, feeling not warm skin but only a chilled, empty pocket of air. Droplets of cold water beaded across my hand and wrist.

"I don't know what to say but I'm sorry."

"I know." Zoe swung her legs and sucked her lower lip into her mouth. She was still the same girl I'd read with, spoken with, watched play, and hugged goodbye nearly every day.

"Why do you keep coming here?" I asked, my voice quavering.

"My sister, Ava, she's only in kindergarten. You have to help her."

My heart lurched, throwing itself against my breastbone.

"What do you mean?"

"He's going to hurt her too. He won't do it the same way, so he won't get caught. He'll come up with some lie that sounds true, and Mom will back him up. She loves him more than she ever loved us. You have to help Ava. He doesn't want any kids, and now that he saw how easy it was to get rid of me, she'll be gone soon."

Again she started sobbing, but I shouted over it, needing to understand.

"What can I do? Call CPS? Talk to her teacher? I don't know enough about her to make a report—"

"No!" The word hit me with the gust of a hurricane, tossing me off the couch and onto the floor, knocking the breath from my lungs. As I struggled to inhale, she calmed herself.

"You need to take her and hide her away. Anywhere. Please believe me, Ms. Wright. You're the only one I trust. Take her and tell her I sent you, then hide her away from him, anywhere. Anywhere is better than home."

My heart still pounding, I rubbed my eyelids, but when I opened them again, she was gone. I didn't sleep at all that night, thinking over everything Zoe had said. By morning, I still hadn't made up my mind.

I showered, dressed, tried to conceal the puffy bags under my eyes, but the makeup only caked into the fine lines, making me look more tired than before. It wasn't until I had parked my car in the lot, an hour before students would arrive per usual, that I realized there was no other choice.

It was easier than expected. I approached in the bustle of morning, twenty-two children unpacking backpacks, coloring morning work, and pestering their teacher. Many parents still walked them to the classroom, kissing their foreheads goodbye and making sure they hung up their coats, so I blended in among the adults. I spotted her right away. She looked nearly identical to her sister.

"Ava?" I asked, but I knew it was her.

"Yeah?"

"You need to come with me real quick, okay?"

"You're not my teacher."

"I know, but I'm Ms. Wright. I was Zoe's teacher. And Mrs. Cantel knows you're coming with me." I made sure to sound casual, almost aloof, like it was the most ordinary request.

"Well, okay," she said, shrugging and following after.

As soon as we were halfway down the hall, she took my hand. It was small and sticky, warm between my fingers. The need to protect her grew with every second I held onto that tiny hand.

She followed to my car without slowing, though she chewed her lip and wouldn't raise her eyes to meet mine. I was an authority figure and I had known her sister. Maybe she knew I was saving her.

When we pulled onto the street, I told her, "Don't worry, Zoe told me everything and sent me to save you."

Ava started to cry. I couldn't tell if she was terrified or grateful. All I could think of was getting to the mountains. We could break into my uncle's cabin, stay for a day or two until I figured things out. I was too exhausted right then to formulate a good plan, but now that I had Ava, I knew Zoe would be at peace. I was making it up to her.

When I looked in the rearview mirror, in the seat next to her weeping, curled-up sister, Zoe smiled at me. I smiled back and stepped on the gas.

The Teachers' Association

Cynthia Gómez

When Esther Díaz pulled up to Eastmont College Prep at 7:30 on Saturday morning, the parking lot was already full, just like in her nightmares, just like in the one she'd had the night before. Her breath felt like it was stuck in her throat, and she pulled out her phone—definitely a Saturday, no events on the school calendar either. She sighed and got her rolling cart out of the trunk. Every car was neatly parked in the lines between each space, and as she walked to the main door she saw that hers was the only one with bumper stickers: "Education Cuts Never Heal," "Make Gilead Fiction Again."

She felt smaller with every room she passed on her way to room 19, which she would be taking over two months into the school year. Every door had the school's motto: "Work Hard and You Can Go Anywhere." Esther knew what her parents would say to that. For decades they had both worked as union organizers for farmworkers, janitors, security guards. People who worked hard every day of their lives, only to end up in the same place. She felt a stab of loneliness.

She relaxed a little when she saw the teacher's lounge in the main building. She knew she'd find a sad old coffeemaker, a stained microwave, and a row of mugs that would all end up in her classroom by the end of the week until she sheepishly returned them late on a Friday. But as she approached the lounge door she could see the shadow of footsteps underneath and hear a low hum that definitely wasn't the sound of percolating liquid. It was more like a chant, an intonation, and she backed away, uncaffeinated. Maybe one of her new colleagues taught yoga. From under the door came a faint, musky scent she couldn't quite place.

She sighed and dragged the cart into room 19. It was bright and spacious, and the faucets and outlets all worked. Her predecessor had apparently left most of his classroom behind. Pocket charts, an arrangement of cheerful pointers, color-coded baskets for markers and pencils and pens. Esther tried not to add up the cost of what must be most of this man's personal collection as she unpacked her own: the silly magnets for science time, the sentence strips she'd arranged alphabetically in a neat little box that Stephen had built for her. She caressed the purple wood and swallowed back tears. She'd already shed enough in the month since he'd left.

"Ms. Díaz. Is this a bad time?"

The figure in the door made Esther's hand steal to her mouth, where she nibbled at the one cuticle that had bravely begun its regrowth. Jessica Gallegos was the Equity and Improvement Lead, as she introduced herself, thanking Esther profusely for stepping in on such short notice. Jessica was wearing a set of gleaming maroon boots, a yellow jumpsuit (how did she keep dry-erase ink off of that?) and a pristine white sweater. On a Saturday. And, Esther noticed with a sinking heart, she was also gorgeous: impossibly smooth brown skin, hair like a sheath of obsidian down her back.

Esther's own daily look had been dress pants and one of the T-shirts she curated and kept in endless supply. At Sobrante Park Community School, where she'd spent her first two years, it was one of her favorite ways to connect with the kids. They'd pepper her with daily questions about where she'd got the one that read "Nerd Nite '09," or who Pedro was and why they should vote for him. For every The Marías or Tiger Army shirt, she'd mix in her dad's Bob Marley ("Emancipate Yourself from Mental Slavery") or her mom's En Vogue ("Free Your Mind and the Rest Will Follow.") Now she felt herself shrinking inside her Converse and jeans.

"Glad to be here." Not quite true, but it was what you were supposed to say. Esther heard the buzzing of her medication alarm, but there was no way she was taking her Xanax in front of this woman. "And I love that jumpsuit. What a cheerful yellow."

"Thank you." Her eyes flicked over Esther's Bikini Kill shirt. "Ninety-eight percent of our students are free or reduced lunch, and we feel it's an equity issue to dress our best. They deserve to see successful adult role models. And it's only fair: after all, we expect them to wear a uniform."

She'd poured ice water over every one of Esther's T-shirts without even trying.

———◦———

Two days later was Monday, Esther's official first day, and she stood on the playground watching the painted line reading "19," waiting for it to fill up with a row of eager third-graders. She'd memorized their names from the cheerful little desk tags she'd made. At the first shrill sounds of the playground bell, three hundred children leapt off the equipment or popped up off the benches, strapped on their backpacks, and lined up along the lines, in complete silence. The nervous smile melted right off Esther's face.

Row by row they filed into the multi-purpose room for Monday morning assembly. Three hundred pairs of feet, making only the necessary noise; three hundred mouths, pressed still. She sat at the end of the third-grade row, wondering if she could sneakily snap a picture and send it to Stephen, but thought better of it. Then she looked up. Esther was the only one sitting in the entire room. She caught the gaze of a teacher with dyed-pink hair standing in the next row; a pair of deep brown eyes flashed upwards, the most subtle of cues, and Esther stuffed her phone back in her blazer and stood. The students were beginning to shuffle now, faces all facing Principal Clark, that red hair rising above her lavender pantsuit. Esther wondered what would happen if she just told her students to go ahead and sit. She bit back the urge. *This is a charter school. They don't have to keep you on. Especially if they start asking why you were still job-hunting in October.* Finally the principal's hands gestured toward the seats and Esther heard nothing but a wave of bodies settling and linoleum scraping against metal feet.

The speech was plenty familiar: lots of "set your sights high" and "care for the community," and the metal taste in her mouth began to dissipate. Then the bodies were again rustling, and again she turned and saw she was the only one in her seat. She must have missed a cue to stand, and now the principal's perfectly made-up face was smiling as she led three hundred voices in her call and response.

"Are we smart?"

"Yes, Principal Clark!"

"Are we going to work harder than yesterday?"

"Yes, Principal Clark!"

"Do we make excuses?"

"No, Principal Clark!"

The metal taste flooded back.

———————◆———————

At lunch Esther found the pink hair again, belonging to a slim woman in a sleeveless blouse who was rearranging a wall of student artwork, at an angle that let Esther admire her muscle tone. The art wall was cheerful and messy, the first sign of either she'd seen in this place.

"I wanted to thank you for your help back there. That was so embarrassing. Definitely not the impression I wanted to make. I'm Ms. Díaz—I mean Esther."

"Ah, you took over Mr. Ramírez's class. Welcome to the salt mines. I'm Bobbie Ma."

Maybe it was something in Bobbie's tone, the way cynicism seeped through the cracks—the first sign that any of these people had cracks at all, that they weren't just made of pressed rayon and mascara and positivity slogans. Or maybe it was just the sound of it, that self-assured low rumbling that Esther had always loved in a woman. But Esther wanted to tumble into those chiseled arms and cry. She had to settle for an invitation to happy hour at the end of the following week, a small group of the newest teachers. "It's usually safe to sneak away after 5 on Fridays," Bobbie told her just before the bell rang, and if that reassurance was supposed to make Esther feel better, it absolutely did not.

———————◆———————

Nor did the offer that came the next day. After lunch, her students were busily coloring in the details on the art project they'd begun on Monday, showing their hopes and dreams for the rest of the year.

They'd acted nervous when she'd explained the assignment, and one little girl (Nathaly, all dark hair and round glasses) raised a hand: "Are we getting graded on this?" Esther had smiled and asked Nathaly to help pass out the markers, and now Nathaly was chattering with her friends at the next table about how to spell the word "scientist." MF Doom's instrumental "Lemon Grass" wafted through the speakers and over the room.

"Ms. Díaz. May I have a word?" came a silky voice beckoning Esther to the door.

Jessica. How the hell did this woman never wear anything shorter than four-inch heels and still manage to sneak up on Esther? The class was staring, markers silent and drying in their hands.

"I know this is only your second day, and so of course you haven't had much time to absorb the curriculum we expect everyone to use here, or the approach that makes us so successful. I think I should come and model a lesson for you and your class tomorrow. Principal Clark will take over my class. Will tomorrow at 10:20 work? Immediately after morning recess."

Esther made herself nod and forced the words "thank you" out of her mouth, feeling like a marionette. A five-foot tall marionette whose black hair was trying to escape from its braid.

On Wednesday she sat in her one suit and watched Jessica line up the members of room 19 in neat rows staring at the Smart Board, where Jessica clicked a remote and a multiple-choice question popped up, something about tablespoons of sugar in a cake. At Sobrante Park, Esther had taught her second-graders how to make pancakes. It was a messy, flour-covered project that taught them all the mathematics of measuring and the use of the imperative mood, because at the end of it they'd each written their own recipe and used it to teach their families. She could almost taste the syrup.

"Now, Ms. Díaz's class," Jessica's voice sang out, sweet as two tablespoons of sugar: "I know that many of the third-graders have difficulty with these kinds of test questions. So, for my special visit. I've given us so many of them. Are we ready to tackle this question?"

"Yes, Ms. Gallegos!"

"Are we smart?"

"Yes, Ms. Gallegos!"

Oh, God. Were they supposed to do this every day? And then, as if Jessica had read her mind: "We lead the students in affirmations before difficult lessons. They need every opportunity to hear how smart they are. We feel it's ..."

Let me guess? An equity issue? Esther forced her face into what she hoped was a thoughtful frown, and onto her notebook she doodled a tiny stick figure, screaming into an inky void. At the end of the "lesson" Jessica presented the classroom with a gift: an aromatherapy diffuser that she plugged in right near Esther's desk. A cloying wave of bergamot and something else she couldn't quite place (clementine?) filled the room, a scent Esther had noted walking past other doors. Now it was here.

"May it bring to your class the success it's brought to all of us," Jessica sang out as she said goodbye, and the children took deep breaths, taking it in.

Next Friday couldn't come fast enough.

———◆———

When Esther finally pushed open the doors of the Laurel Lounge, she was more than ready to take her place with a gaggle of exhausted teachers gossiping over their beers. Instead, there was only Bobbie, perched on a stool and showing off wonderfully smooth legs, and Angie Chávez, who had technically a day's seniority on Bobbie; she'd been hired in a rush after the school had enrolled too many first-graders.

"Aren't the others coming?" Esther hoped her disappointment hadn't leaked into her voice.

Bobbie let out a long sigh. "Rivera and Bittner said they had to get up early. There's a TA meeting in the morning."

"A what?"

"They haven't talked to you yet about the Teachers' Association?" Bobbie asked.

"You mean like the union? I thought charter schools don't usually have them."

Angie's black eyes darted aside at this comment, and she took an urgent pull on her drink before she answered.

"No. Clark started it back when she came here. Thirteen years ago. This meets every Saturday at 7:30."

"Every what the fuck?"

As soon as the words left Esther's mouth, she wanted to pull them back in. Angie hadn't said, *"They* meet every Saturday," and Esther might have just insulted one of her few allies here. But Angie smiled and pulled out her phone, to a photo of two grinning boys, about eight and ten, both with their mother's curly hair and slightly goofy expression. "I only get them on weekends now, so I'm glad nobody's asked me to join yet."

"They can't make you, right?" Esther tried not to let either of her parents creep into her tone just then.

"No"—Bobbie's voice echoed in her lemonade glass as she emptied it—"But, as you said, there's no union here. I'm just glad I've got the new baby excuse. We'll see how long that lasts."

"Wait, you don't mean everyone else is in it?"

Just then the bartender came to ask if they wanted any specials before happy hour closed. They all shook their heads, and Esther chugged her watery margarita and slid a twenty across the bar. For days she'd been looking forward to breathing just a little, to loosening the tightness in her spine she'd been carrying all week. And now she could feel the wire twist inside her, tighter than ever.

She was in her classroom early the next morning, setting up the rest of her library and putting up a batch of student art; by ten she still had hours to go but her head was screaming for more coffee, and so she gathered up the week's worth of mugs and headed for the teachers' lounge. The hallway was chilly and dark, but lit by a faint glow coming from underneath the lounge door. The same cloying smell that filled her room spilled out from under the door; the same low hum from the week before echoed into the hall. But now there was something familiar, the rising and falling voices forming a pattern she could almost make out. She leaned closer to the door, trying to recognize individual voices in the hum.

And then the doorknob began to move. Esther scrambled around the corner and ducked into the supply room just in time, as her colleagues were filing out of the lounge. She watched them through the blinds as they left one by one. Silent. No grateful yammering at their phones, no "Hey, can I ask you about your student Miles?" All of them staring straight ahead, their hands resting perfectly at their sides, all walking at the same pace, and Esther could hear the classroom doors shutting one after the other, like the metronomic beat of a song.

All day she tried only to see the tasks in front of her: the homework to grade, the vocabulary wall to redo. But behind her eyes those eyes were staring, those feet walking all of a pace.

It was dark by the time she could feed her homework packets to the shiny new copier, the last task of the day. She thought of the collapsing machine at Sobrante Park, the art projects she could have made with all the mangled flyers and worksheets spit out by the beast. This thing was humming along, and in that hum she could hear high-heeled boots clacking, the soft scritch of a red pen flying over piles of exams.

In the corner of the supply room was a shelf with spiral-bound yearbooks, a staff group photo at the end of each, and she thumbed through them while the machine stapled and stacked. The room was thick with bergamot and that other scent—she'd decided it was too musky to be clementine—and the fluorescent lights glared down on the photos.

What the hell? This had to be wrong.

Every name, every face, of every teacher, was the same, year after year. The faces getting older, of course, a little more wrinkled, hair a little more gray, but the same. Every once in a long while a face would disappear from one year to the next and be replaced with a new one. That was the other thing. Each new face was shining and bright the first year it appeared. And then the next? Something was gone from their eyes. As if the light inside had been stamped out and replaced with an Edison bulb.

———◦———

"So you're saying your new school is neat, clean, and well-run, and that the staff has better retention than most private schools—and this is a problem why?" Esther knew she shouldn't have confided in her roommate Zoe, who'd been unemployed for weeks and had never taught anyway. But there'd been no one else home when Esther crawled in at a quarter to eight, face flushed and hands covered in Sharpie ink. It was still too soon to text Stephen. She didn't know Bobbie well enough. Her parents were in some corner of Guatemala with great politics and bad cell phone reception. Esther slumped over the kitchen table.

"Come on; I'll make you some tea. Bergamot?" Zoe reached for the kettle, and stopped when she saw Esther's face.

"Is that ... not good?"

Esther grabbed a box of peanut butter cookies and headed to her room.

———◆———

Bobbie was out all the next week; she took her kids on a field trip and then came down with the flu. So Esther had no one to tell about the nearly twice-daily visits from Jessica, or the little notes she left ("I wonder if your students are doing enough affirmations? We find that they are so helpful!!" or "I wonder if they should be doing so much unstructured reading?") Sometimes Jessica brought a "gift" that Esther had to smile and accept: refill cartridges for the diffuser, a set of motivational posters, so many and so big that Esther had to take down her favorite Biko quote: "The greatest weapon in the hand of the oppressor is the mind of the oppressed."

———◆———

On Saturday, Esther got to school at 7:00, so she could get to the supply room before anyone else. She heard the sound of teachers settling into the lounge, but nobody touched the supply room door while she took pictures of every one of the staff photos. Maybe she could show them to Bobbie, maybe to Stephen; hell, maybe a curious reporter would want to write an inspirational piece about this school with its skyrocketing test scores, long wait list, and near-perfect teacher retention. Why was it that nobody had? She tucked her phone in her backpack and went to refill her water bottle in the alcove by the front door.

Then she saw Angie Chávez in the hallway. There was something wrong with her face. Her mouth was stretched, as if she'd been crying, and she was walking towards the teacher's lounge door as if inside it lay her own nightmares. She even turned, looked behind her twice, and started back the way she'd come. Then the door opened. "Ms. Chávez! We were getting worried about you." Angie caught Esther's eyes before Principal Clark ushered her inside, her brown skin blanched and pale. The principal's smile stretched wider when she saw Esther, and her perfectly manicured hand reached out. "Ms. Díaz. Have you come to join us this morning? What good news!"

Esther fled. She was panting by the time she reached her car and started up the engine, and before she even knew where she was going she was pulling up to Sobrante Park Community School. There was a tiny sprinkling of cars in the lot, and she knew one of her former colleagues might walk by as she sat crumpled over the steering wheel, tears dripping onto her blouse. No matter; they all knew what had happened. Every day they all walked by the sapling planted in the yard in memory of Josué, her second-grader who brought his dad's gun to school and pulled it out of his backpack in the cafeteria, so he could show his friends his awesome new toy. It had taken four months of therapy before she could imagine stepping inside a school again, by which time she was desperately ready to take the first opening she found: Eastmont College Prep.

That night she dreamed of a building as large as an airplane hangar, filled with rows of children lined up along unmoving conveyor belts. At the head of each row was a smiling teacher, and every smiling face was the same—except for Angie's, and Bobbie's, and Esther's own. From a podium at the front of the room Principal Clark descended, bearing a jar of salve that she smoothed over Angie's face, and her features melted away until they matched everyone else's. Then Angie's hand descended on a lever and the belt moved, pulling the students towards the corrugated metal door, chains rattling and hinges creaking as it rolled up. Esther tried to warn Bobbie, but all that came out of her mouth were the lyrics to "Redemption Song." Esther couldn't see what waited on the other side of the opening door, but she knew she had to warn the children. As she drew closer she saw that every one of them was Josué, their uniform shirts wet with blood.

Monday morning the recess bell summoned the students, silent as always on their painted lines, and as Angie led her class into the multi-purpose room, Esther found that metal taste flooding back. Angie's hair was straightened and pulled into a tight bun at the back of her neck, and her eyes focused on something Esther couldn't quite see. When Principal Clark gestured for everyone to sit, she beckoned to Angie with a crooked finger, and Angie rose and took the podium, her voice light and sweet.

"Are we smart?"

"Yes, Ms. Chávez!"

As the affirmation repeated, Principal Clark's eyes darted over the room. Esther could have sworn she could see the pattern: Rivera, Bittner, Chávez. That left only Ma. And Díaz, of course.

———◆○◆———

Recess brought rain that lasted until late in the afternoon, keeping Esther inside with her students all day. She finally found Bobbie just before five, feeding tests into the maw of the copier. Esther shut the door firmly behind her and took a timid step towards her friend. She knew how she would sound as soon as she started to tell it: Angie's face that morning, all the teachers walking in step, the photos, her nightmares, those eyes moving in a pattern over the room.

"Bobbie, doesn't Eastmont seem a little ... different from the other schools you've worked at?"

Bobbie glanced at the door.

"Not here. Listen, I can't make happy hour this week, but are you free Saturday afternoon? I'm going to see if I can invite the union rep from my old school. He's been around a long time and he's pretty sharp."

Esther nodded and just then Jessica walked in, her eyes flickering over them both.

"Ms. Ma. Ms. Díaz. So good to see your dedication. Will you be long at the copier?"

Esther gazed at her hands and counted: five days. Five more days to hold it all in.

———◆○◆———

On Saturday Esther got to the Laurel Lounge at a few minutes to four and ordered a virgin margarita for Bobbie and a rum and coke for herself. The ice cubes softened and shrunk as the clock swept on to 4:30 and her texts to Bobbie got no reply, and by the time she finally paid her bill at 5:00 they had disappeared entirely, leaving the drink watery and thin.

———◦———

Esther knew what she'd see on Monday morning when Bobbie arrived. And it was all wrong the second she stepped through her friend's classroom door. Gone were the overstuffed reading chairs, the art wall, even Bobbie's pink hair. And Bobbie's voice was wrong too, that sardonic drawl now a light sing-song that carried across the room.

"Ms. Díaz! I'm so sorry I couldn't make it on Saturday. I got here at 7:30 and I just had so much to do. You know how it goes. Here, would you kindly help me straighten this?" She gestured to the Behavior Chart on the wall, fresh out of the laminator and still warm.

———◦———

Friday afternoon, Esther sat in Principal Clark's office and delivered the speech she'd honed all week. She'd had plenty of time to practice; she'd slept maybe eight hours in five days. The principal's face was so impassive as Esther spoke that for a second she wondered if she'd actually said any of her speech, or only meant to.

"Ms. Díaz, you understand that the State may revoke your credential if you leave without being released?"

"Can't you see that this just isn't a good fit? Mr. Ramírez must have thought so too."

For a second Principal Clark's eyes flashed what looked like the color of jade. Then she lifted a mug to her perfectly lipsticked mouth, and Esther could see the green liquid inside, smell the tea.

"I will consider releasing you, if you are really unhappy here. But you'll stay until we find a replacement, won't you?"

Esther pictured a room of little faces, the light fading from their eyes each day as a string of substitutes paraded through. Nathaly, who had started begging her mother to go to science camp; César, who stayed in at lunch time so he could read his way through Esther's books.

"Of course."

"I know you've never joined the TA, but maybe you could come this Saturday? It will be such a shock to our little community, losing two teachers in one classroom in a semester. It would be nice if you came to say goodbye."

Those voices humming in unison, those bodies streaming silently from the room. And yet this woman held Esther's teaching career in her hand.

"I'll see if I can cancel my appointment." The appointment she had with a box of cookies and every depressing Depeche Mode song she could find.

The principal's phone buzzed. "I'm so sorry, Ms. Díaz; would you excuse me just a moment?"

She stepped into her adjoining office and Esther had to will her chest not to shudder, the tears to stay safely inside. *Almost there. Almost.*

Just then a text came in: *Hey, it's Bobbie. So sorry again for flaking! Michelle and I have been going through it and the kiddo's kept us up teething and I've been such a zombie. Dying to hear how the salt mines have been treating you. Have they started the helpful notes yet?*

Esther could feel her thoughts doubling, tripling back on themselves. Was the real Bobbie still in there somewhere? Maybe it took more than one meeting, at least for some? What if that chanting was less of an initiation and more of a test? Maybe Mr. Ramírez had failed. And maybe ... maybe Esther was just exhausted and traumatized and raw and this place was bad bootstrap pedagogy and test-prep drills, nothing more?

———◦———

Back in her classroom, as she loaded up her bag with papers and her grading pens, a text came in from Stephen: *Hey. Is it too soon? How you doing? How's the new job?*

She felt a warmth spread through her chest, a lightness she hadn't felt in so long, and she typed back: *So much to tell you Job is a story and a half, but I'm actually leaving it soon. You around tmw? I said I would go to this meeting in the morning, but I'm just going to put in an appearance. I should be finished around eight. And then I'll be free.*

Auxiliary, Supplementary, Inessential

Christi Nogle

T he two newer adjuncts are sharing their teaching dreams. I look up, smile, and go back to my notebook, pretending I am writing something important.

It's not that I haven't written about teaching dreams before. There was even one that I sold to a little horror magazine years ago. Only lightly fictionalized, that one, if fictionalizing is even what you can call the process of filling lacunae in a recalled dream so it reads as a gapless thing.

Gapless, I write in my notebook and doodle spirals all around the word. There's only me and the newer adjuncts in the faculty room now, and it's cold in here. I could sleep if there wasn't a professional development meeting about to start. I love this smelly little room.

In the story I sold to the magazine, the teacher was taken over by a mindless parasitic thing that stole her body. Other starts didn't become stories. One was of a final exam I had not written, that I tried to make up and write on the board on the spot, the students tensed before me with their sharpened pencils raised. Ready, I thought, to hurl them into me.

The classrooms L-shaped or U-shaped so that you could not see the students at either end and when you were serving some of them, the others revolted, so desperate for your eyes on them, so desperate to smell your breath …

There are more people in the room now, and somehow the conversation has infected them so that all of them speak of their teaching dreams (none so vivid as my own). The smallest part of my own dreams I express here in the faculty room among our snacks of carrots and of hummus and pita, artichoke-spinach dip, and grapes. So sleep-sick and red-eyed, all of us, because we care so very much. Because we give of ourselves.

Taste of my flesh, I think, *taste of my vegetables and dips.*

I speak some part of a dream as we wait for the rest of our colleagues. *Icebreaking*, I write as I speak, and draw skulls all around it. I speak of clear plastic tunnels we must climb through on our way from classroom to classroom in the dreams, how we must press and slide against each other in these intestinal passageways.

This is starting to feel a little dangerous, I think, with dread and glee. Boldly I crunch someone's cookie, a dry and vegan cookie from their home. I come down wrong on a bad molar and feel the crack, the icy pressure of bone shards. My teeth are bad on one side and worse on the other, no health insurance because that is for the full-times though there aren't any full-times anymore.

We adjuncts teach three classes one semester and four the next, which makes seven-eighths of full time. Though full-time does not exist, they are talking about making it five and five so that then part-time could be four and five. The tenures teach only two and one or two and three to leave time for their crucial research, but there aren't many tenures left and the ones who are left, you look at them and they look away. Except now, with this talk of dreams, the sallow tenure sitting here in our group does not quite look away. Not quite. She's listening for something, listening closely to me. I feel it.

I cannot shut up. I speak of my dreams with the dread and glee coming up closer to my skin, burning my face. I am not looking down at my notebook now; I look at the colleagues, but the flush of it has gone all the way into my eyes. I see nothing.

After the icebreaker, snacks and meeting and everything, when we are supposed to go sit in our cars and grade papers until class, the tenure asks me—me!—to come to her office. Her overheated office smelling of Trader Joe's lemon lotion and moldy old books, she asks me, and I go.

Am I being let go? I wonder, but no, surely they do that in late August before classes start. The day before classes start, I imagine, they send you a text. Or not. You just show up for your class all bleary-eyed from finalizing the syllabus and there's some other person teaching. You run toward the office to see if there's been some mistake and a security guard tackles you on the way, hurls you onto the sidewalk.

I remember standing at the copier making my hundreds of pages of syllabi when a tenure came to the doorway with her papers, saw me, sighed heavily and said *Aw, shit* before trudging back to her office. Hogging the copier when she had just that one little thing to print for her nine or ten students, how rude of me.

Maybe their research is not so crucial after all, I sometimes wonder, but no, that's too unkind.

I remember a male tenure, during a department meeting, reasoning out why the full-times each ought to have only four-tenths instead of four-eighths of a vote in department matters. My, wasn't he passionate, eloquent. This was back when there were full-times here. Oh, how many years ago was that?

"An opportunity," this tenure whispers now, looking deep into my eyes. Mine. Hers are green and gold. I love her for seeing me.

"An opportunity? For me?" I say all breathless.

"Experimental, but *really* promising," she says, passing a brochure across the desk. "I think you'd be perfect."

But this can't be, I'm thinking, barely able to focus on the brochure. More classes? A new program? Heart about to burst. *Full time*? Rainbows and fireworks strobe in my mind, and dollar signs, a shiny new car, a bright white dental implant in a smiling dentist's fingers like a diamond ring, but then it all recedes with her next words.

"The programs are separate. Seven-eighths time here—or nine-tenths once our proposal goes through—and up to seven-eighths time there, Maris. No benefits, of course, but you'd make more and who knows ... if it all works out ..."

———◦———

I lie in bed thinking I ought not to have been so rude. It was unexpected, that was all.

"A month's pay?" I asked the silver-haired lady in the program office, all my anger and bafflement unrestrained. "How can that be?"

She said, "What does parking cost, in the other program?"

The building was only a stone's throw from campus, but it seemed another country. Everything so vague and echoey. I figured in my head and said, "Parking costs two weeks' pay, a little less."

She shrugged.

Two weeks for just a parking space, and here she was offering a bed for only twice that. More than a bed, too: a nice little locker, a shower down the hall. Oh, I'd been ungrateful.

"I'm so sorry," I said, signing the form, and she only kept that disgusted look on her face like she thought I wasn't sorry at all, but I was. I am sorry still, lying here fretting about it.

"Five minutes to sleep cycle; put away devices, lights on," says a voice in the wall behind the bed. My devices are all in the locker already. I am a rule follower.

A researcher and assistant come in. The assistant administers the shot with the researcher directing. A cabinet behind the bed opens and red-and-blue cords and tubes tumble out, just barely in my line of sight. One of the people hooks me up, but by then I am only half aware. The lights go off and they are silhouettes going out the door. "Lights out," says the voice from the wall, some long time later.

I stretch into the dream, wake into the dream.

————◦————

Sitting at a conference table in a blurred and shapeless room, I begin in a freeze, in panic. The faces hover in and out like the earliest memories of childhood, leering faces over your crib. For a second I am sure I *am* in a crib, but then a husky-voiced woman says, "She's stabilizing. She's doing fine." The woman's sitting close like people used to do sometimes, years ago. She rubs my back in strong slow strokes. Her face is bright and friendly, her curly hair blurring away into the room. "I'm your mentor, Judy. Just stay here. Don't slip away."

"Where are we?" I say, and my voice echoes. The other faces around the table are too far away to see.

"Orientation," says Judy.

"The room," I gasp. She's cloyingly close, and everything else too far away. There's not enough air.

"I think it's a composite of what we all expect to see," she says, looking around. "Some things are like that here. Don't worry." She has her arm around my shoulder, squeezes me in toward her.

The meeting goes on. I do not understand what people say. Sometimes I ask Judy, but she only hushes me and smiles again. From far across the table, I make out the word "accreditation."

A woman rushes in, says we're about to miss the Orientation Parade, but the meeting goes on. I feel the tension at that, everyone must. They're missing the parade, but they keep droning on. They cannot stop themselves.

Finally people begin gathering things left on the table. Someone rises.

"And let's not forget Maris, our new adjunct," Judy says, and they drop their things again to clap. A standing ovation, short but enthusiastic. Each face comes clear on their way out the door, and each one shakes my hand in that warm way people used to, years ago.

"We're all adjuncts here," says Judy as we follow them down the hall. She's holding my hand.

At the real college's orientation day, we hear speeches by administrators and pick up a sack lunch to eat in the quad, but here where money is no object, the entertainment's far finer. A feast of succulent meats, fruits, and cakes is piled high on a long table. Live music and decorated horses. Tiny parade floats bloat and then hover up into the sky. Oh, it's *that* kind of parade!

"Let's go," says Judy, leading me into a basket, and soon we are floating over the campus and over a shimmering city, then canyons, desert, mountains.

I wake, shower, go to morning classes, grade, and eat stale crackers in my car before afternoon classes. It's seven o'clock when I get to my apartment to pack a change of clothes and watch a little Netflix before I have to get back to the bed-cubicle for lights out. Halfway through the movie I remember tomorrow's night class, so I pack up another change of clothes. There won't be time to come home at all tomorrow. It will be Thursday before I can return. I'm glad I never got a cat after all.

I look back on the apartment with nostalgia, like it's already gone. My bookcases with all their yellow "Used" stickers from the campus bookstore, family photo albums unopened for years, my sunken-in spot before the television. One Philodendron sits on the kitchen sill, already drooping.

On Zoom, Judy's curls blur into the background just like they do in our dreams—or in our late-night shifts, as she says I should call them. I Zoom, grade, and watch Netflix sprawled on my cubicle-bed between classes now. I've gathered a new mini-fridge and the coffee maker from home as well as a stack of my best school clothes.

"Still keeping the apartment, though? I really don't think you need to," says Judy.

We love you. Don't you love us? is how she put it during our shift last night. *Don't you love our students?*

"The students are wonderful. It isn't that," I say. I don't know if they're wonderful; it's just something you say.

I speak of the space where I met them for class last night, something conjured from my old honors program building so long ago. The dream-building was sunk in the ground like a burrow, with three musty rooms in a row, the students all chilling on loveseats and ottomans and huddled by fireplaces. I wandered back and forth trying to get them corralled into one room so I could begin, but it never happened. We never came together, never had a lecture at all, but maybe we were happy enough just trying.

"In the dream classes, I forget what subject it is I even teach," I say.

"And how does that feel?" asks Judy. Taking in my expression, she nods. "It feels so good, doesn't it?"

Maybe the subject itself is the source of failure, of striving, of suffering. No subject, no worries. In the late-night classes, without content, I can merely keep an eye on the students, which is really all anyone expects. Keep my eyes roving from one to another to another, and everyone will be happy. Even me.

"They're only getting elective credits anyway, while we work through the kinks," Judy says. "Don't sweat it."

———— ◆ ————

I let the apartment go and sold my car, which meant the expenses for rent, gas, parking, and car insurance could be redirected into marketplace health and dental insurance with enough left over for a cafeteria plan.

Funny, though. When I went to the dentist to finally get things fixed, they said my new card would cover only a thousand dollars of work, that the rest would have to go on payments.

And I was not doing well in my daylight classes, not like I used to. I'd forgotten too much of my subject. I tried to do what I did in the late-night classes: milling around, letting my eyes rove so all would see they were being seen. It didn't work the same in waking life.

An out-of-body feeling would come over me in class and I'd talk straight to the students about myself. I'd tell them what an adjunct was and how many of us there were. I'd tell them the definitions they might read were all wrong. We weren't retirees or what have you; this was all we knew how to do, and the institution needed us, but it refused to make us full-time so that we were somehow never real.

I'd say how I had started vague and weak like they were now, and through education had been built up and honed. I'd developed compassion, bravery, organizational and time-management skills, people skills, deep knowledge of and passion for my subject. Though I couldn't remember what it was anymore, I knew that was true. I felt it deep down and remembered the nights studying and enthusiasm for anything to do with that subject. Conferences, papers, speeches, video projects, and all.

I had been made into something wonderful and then I had been thrown away.

All the time saying this I was somewhat outside myself judging the room, gauging their responses. I was thinking they thought me pathetic, that they would laugh and jeer. The more sensitive and vulnerable of them would be thinking I was taking my great luck and privilege for granted. Here I was, someone who had achieved so much more than they had, and I didn't value or deserve it. The affluent, bullying types would sense my weakness and turn away in disgust.

But the response when it came was not that. It was anger, hatred from all. I saw how they held sharpened pencils, how all the pencils raised at once.

From up by the ceiling, I watched them advance and take their turns, each one stabbing only two or three or four times before stepping back to let the others in. Such teamwork!

The blood pooled around the openings, and then as more pencils violated the same places again and again, the blood began to flow rich and red. Down my arms, soaking my tweed skirt, gliding onto the floor like dark oil with a skim of froth at its edge.

One punched through my cheek, impaling my gums, and that hurt more than anything.

I didn't cry or fight. I only kept speaking through the pain, my eyes roving from face to face. I was still trying to teach them something.

Tenures and other adjuncts came in from the hall, watching a moment and then taking their turns too with fountain pens and such, and still I kept speaking. I knew I had nothing to say, but I couldn't stop. Not until I was drained out could I stop, not until I had stumbled and gurgled and brought a desk down with me to the floor, my cheek sliding along in the cooling blood.

I was really up in the ceiling, not there on the floor. I watched the people milling around.

"Does this mean class is canceled?" one guy said. My sallow tenure, rolling her eyes at that, happened to spot me up in the ceiling. She smirked and looked away quickly, but another one saw, and another. They started to stack up the desks.

"It felt so real," I tell Judy on Zoom, "and it covered so much time too. When I woke up, I knew I hadn't gotten attacked, but I thought my apartment was gone, and my car. I might have never realized the car wasn't still there except I got a call from security. Someone broke the windows and it got towed."

"Maybe you'll do those things, maybe today. Let that apartment go at least," she says.

"We're getting accredited, aren't we?"

She doesn't answer my question, but her beaming smile tells a lot. "You can't go off into your own dreams anymore. You can't be absent like that again."

"I'm sorry," I say.

"That car got attacked even if you didn't. Someone sensed weakness and struck it, then someone else saw it broken and towed it away."

"I should go get it," I say.

"Forget it. It's gone."

———— ◆ ————

Who are they, I wonder sometimes, these people who signed up for late-night school? They are blurred at the edges, their clothing too vague to assess. Only their faces come to me clearly, and they look just like anyone else. There isn't time to get to know them, really, but I pretend I know them well.

Tonight we've met in a cool, sun-dappled orchard, and while some sit under trees dozing and flirting, others pick apples and climb short ladders to reach for bright clusters of cherries. I made this space. It isn't vague like the conference room because they give up their will and let me lead.

I weave between the trees lecturing. "At first glance it might appear ... but a closer look reveals ..." I say, and there is no content to it. I say, "Some of the earliest theories of ... maintain that ... and over time researchers began to ask ..." and a group of three young women come with fruit held in the bottoms of their blouses. Laughing, they stuff cherries in my mouth to shut me up.

Are the late-night students here just for this, just to be children?

The flesh is crisp and sweet as apples in my mouth, and suddenly Judy is there rubbing my back saying, "Stay with us. Good. Nothing matters, just that you stay with us."

—•◦•—

I show up to my eight a.m. class and there is a plump young man standing at my lectern. I turn toward the office, glimpse the security guard waiting in shadows a few doors down. If I go for the office, he'll head me off, tackle me, hurl me onto the sidewalk, and though it feels unfair—I haven't done anything wrong—I turn the other way. I burst out into the cool spring morning. Yellow and salmon-colored daffodils play in the breeze, and I head toward my car to eat crackers. The car is not there, of course.

Back in my cubicle, a knock comes. No one has knocked here before.

It's the silver-haired lady. It seems the cubicles are meant for our late-night shifts and not for full-time living. She sees numerous violations. Personal items outside the locker, appliances, "filthy, filthy" laundry. She's marking things down on a legal pad.

"Let's just call Judy," I say. She's said to call if I ever need help.

On Zoom, she's happier than I've ever seen her. "There's no problem at all," she says.

The silver-haired woman says, "Now just one minute ..."

"It's done! Full accreditation. Maris is full time. We all are." Something, some gesture of a hand breaks through her blurred background. My blood runs cold.

I realize that Judy is in bed. A researcher or an assistant is prepping her arm for the sleepy-shot, and the red-and-blue cords and tubes tumble down. It can't be eight-thirty in the morning.

"Oh, I didn't realize," says the silver-haired woman, turning on me with the first pleasant look I've ever caught from her. My eyes drift down to her legal pad and catch a few cruel words. I bet she's sorry for writing them now.

Her phone is vibrating in her pocket. Her desk phone trills from the other room.

Behind my bed, a voice says, "Five minutes to sleep cycle; put away devices, lights on."

"It's happening so fast," she says. The delight in her voice makes me think of my long-dead grandma. "You better get your pajamas on and I'll see who can set you up." She's moving toward the hall.

All I can think of are the daffodils, the clash of yellow and salmon, the breeze on them. I go to the door. I think I will shut it for privacy, but something has me. Some panic, some flash of rare courage. I check that the hall is clear, and never would I have guessed I'd do it, but I *run*.

The Consultant's Hand

D. Matthew Urban

Your new office lies at the end of a long, bright hallway. As I escort you there, I sense your unease mounting. Your eyes dart left and right, peering through doorway after doorway into rooms where desks sit unoccupied, lecterns stand empty, spotless chalkboards glow like virgin meadows lit by fluorescent suns. No words on the chalkboards, no books on the shelves. No students, no instructors. Only stillness and emptiness and the lights' perpetual hum.

"Hasn't the semester started?" you say. "Aren't classes in session?"

"Yes, since two weeks ago," I say. "Which, of course, made us all the more anxious to fill the position as quickly as possible. I can't tell you how grateful we are that you were able to join us on such short notice. After Professor Tryon's abrupt departure, we thought we might have to cancel her classes. Reshuffle enrollments, refund tuition. An administrative nightmare."

Our footsteps echo along the speckled tile, coming back to us from the end of the hallway as if we were there already, walking toward ourselves. I read the questions scrawled in your darting eyes, fear's unmistakable signature in your quivering mouth. I smile and give you a reassuring pat on the shoulder. There is nothing to be afraid of. Soon you will know all.

If you'd joined us only a year ago, instead of peace and tranquility you'd have found chaos, the typical disarray of an understaffed humanities department at a small and unprestigious public college. Professors harried to madness by budget cuts, sleep-deprived students rushing from class to job to home to job to class, adjuncts staring hollow-eyed into the void of no future … no offense, of course! And trapped in that madhouse, swirling in that whirlpool, you would have found me, an assistant professor struggling to keep my grip on the lowest rung of the golden ladder. I was the second-to-last non-contingent hire before the university began cutting the department's tenure lines. The last was Professor Tryon.

We've reached your office. I hand you the key. "Welcome to the department!" I say.

…

"Hmm. Are you sure it won't open? Try again. Try jiggling the knob."

…

Well, that old fool in the department office must have given me the wrong key. Never mind, I know where all the keys are kept. Come with me.

Yes, in those days I was a mere assistant professor. Not as lowly as some—how do you adjuncts survive, I wonder?—but hardly an exalted personage. Hardly the head of the department. How did I rise so far in so short a time, when the wheels of academia turn as slowly as dreams revolving in a dead god's brain? Simple. I seized the initiative. I saw a chance, and I took it.

I recall last year's first departmental meeting as clearly as my daughter's darling face. Needless to say, I had no idea what that hour would bring. None of us did, except old Professor Casimir, the department head at the time. The rest of us expected nothing but the usual tedious bickering over course loads and committee appointments. I remember Professor Tryon nudging my shoulder as she took the seat next to mine at the long table in the seminar room—that seminar room there, the one we're passing now. "Are you ready to be ... enraptured?" she whispered, rolling her eyes toward the head of the table where Professor Casimir sat, rehearsing his opening remarks under his breath.

I can almost hear those words now, Professor Tryon's whisper taking shape from the hum of the fluorescent lights. *Are you ready to be enraptured?*

Professor Casimir's remarks began with the standard announcement of catastrophe. More budget cuts brewing, state legislators huddled like warlocks around a cauldron conjuring famine. The standard phrases followed—"tighten our belts," "do more with less." Next to me, Professor Tryon let out an almost-silent groan. I felt her breath, soft and warm on my cheek. My mind wandered from the meeting.

When I refocused a few moments later, Professor Casimir was saying, "The administration realizes that previous reductions have left our resources strained, and that the expected cuts will make it even more difficult for us to fulfill our educational mission. They have generously decided to assist us by ..."

"Reducing their own salaries?" someone said from the far end of the room, their voice disguised with a cough. I hid my smile behind my hand. Professor Tryon chuckled.

"... by offering the services of a consultant," Professor Casimir continued. "A consultant who specializes in this sort of thing."

Behind me, the door of the seminar room swung open. A chilly draft from the hallway raised goosebumps on the back of my neck.

"And here he is!" Professor Casimir said.

The consultant strode to the head of the table, moving as if wrapped in a holy nimbus of certainty. His face was sharp and spare, his dark suit perfectly tailored. Absolute confidence glared from the round lenses of his wire-rimmed glasses.

"You may expect I've come to teach you how to squeeze blood from a stone," he said. "How to *do more with less*." Repeating the hackneyed phrase, the consultant shot a scornful glance at Professor Casimir over the tops of his glittering lenses. The department head seemed to shrivel in shame under that gaze, to wither before our eyes.

"Well," the consultant said, "I'm not here to teach you that. I'm not here to teach you anything. You're the teachers, not me. You're the heroes, and I am your humble servant. I'm here to help you realize what you already know. There's no need to squeeze blood from a stone, because stone itself is nothing but blood. There's no need to do more with less, because you can do everything with nothing."

Yes, this way, down the stairs. All the way down to the bottom of things. Why they keep the keys in the basement I'll never know.

Except for Professor Casimir, who'd long learned to dance to whatever tune the administration cared to whistle, we were all pretty skeptical of the consultant at first. I remember Professor Tryon imitating his oily smirk and preacher's voice over dinner with me and my daughter, leaving us howling with laughter. My daughter loved Professor Tryon. Almost as much as...well, never mind.

But you already realized I was in love with Professor Tryon, didn't you? Of course you did. The bit about her breath on my cheek was something of a giveaway. And after all, you're a literature teacher.

Interpretation is your business, your passion. You love to unravel clues. You can't resist a puzzle. Any more than Professor Tryon could.

Anyway, we laughed and made fun and were skeptical. *Just a bunch of hot air, another snake oil salesman peddling the same old austerity bullshit.* So we thought, at first.

Until the trainings started.

We assembled for the first training in the same seminar room where the consultant had given his spiel. The chair at the head of the table sat empty. I had a slight headache that made the glare of the fluorescent lights seem harsher than usual, their hum more piercing. In the seat next to me, Professor Tryon rolled her eyes and moaned with boredom. That breath on my cheek again. My head spun. I closed my eyes.

When I opened them, the consultant was sitting at the head of the table, smiling his holy smile. A book lay open in front of him, a thick old hardcover with yellowed pages. *Middlemarch*, maybe, or *The Mysteries of Udolpho*. He raised a spread hand, let it hover palm-down above the tome.

"You're all scholars, lovers of the humanities," he said. "You've all been accustomed to regard a book as something sacred. When you see your students hunched over their phones, watching little videos and giggling at shitposts instead of relishing the masterpieces of literature, your tender hearts ache with pity. *I have to save them*, you think. *I have to give them an education.*"

Above the book, his hand began to quiver. My headache contracted into a single point of agony like a drill boring out from inside my brain. The glaring lights flashed on his fingernails. The hum rose to a banshee wail.

"In the back of your mind, though," he said, "you know it's only a matter of time. Books, literature, the humanities, all of it—it's fading. Draining out of the world like oil out of a cracked pipeline. What you've spent your life on, all the passions of your heart ... it's all nothing. You know this. In the back of your mind. At the bottom of your soul."

His hand shook and flailed as if he were having a seizure, but his face was totally calm, his voice smooth and placid. I looked into his eyes, blazing with holy truth behind lenses that reflected the fluorescent lights' empty glow, and I knew he was right. It was all nothing. My life, my years of work, for nothing.

"That is what I've come to help you realize," he said. "And that is what you will help your students realize. Because it's not only books that are fading. Books are like the first leaf of autumn, whirled down beautifully in a gentle breeze. And what comes after autumn? You know, don't you, what kind of storm is on its way. At the bottom of your soul, you know it's all over. Everything is draining away. This world is a cracked pipeline, a tanker run aground, vomiting the dregs of our lives all over the wretched landscape of a soiled universe. And your students know that, too. Just look in their eyes and see how deeply they know that this putrid world, this monstrous wreck, is their only inheritance. They know, but they don't realize. And you will help them realize. You will grant them the gift of realizing the truth of humanity. A true humanities education!"

His hand danced and shone, a knot of flames in the wailing light, and he brought it down like a comet of destruction to crash into the dull surface of the long table. Nothing impeded its fall. The book had disappeared, dissolved into nothingness.

And here's the basement. Watch your head, the ceiling's low down here. The key room's just this way. What? No, I don't need to get a key from the custodian. There's no key to the key room. Remember that. The key room is never locked, and anyone who dares can go right in. Keep that in mind, and you'll go far.

That was our first training, but it wasn't the last. As the consultant imparted his techniques to us, my colleagues and I began to acquire something of his quiet assurance. I'd spent my whole career thrashing in a sticky web of words—wrestling with difficult texts, weltering through student papers, grinding out lectures, articles, proposals—and every volume that evaporated at my touch was a loosening of the awful web, a blessed silence wrenched from cacophony. Most of the faculty felt the same. A new calm tempered the department's air of scurrying anxiety.

By the spring, we'd all learned the knack of making books vanish. Some of the more talented faculty had moved on from dissolving individual copies of books to obliterating the texts themselves, wiping whole novels and poems out of existence as if they'd never been written, and then on from literary texts to movies, songs, albums, TV shows. No false modesty here—I was the most talented of all. By winter break, I'd erased three Victorian triple-decker novels, two early Rolling Stones B-sides, and a beloved masterpiece of Finnish cinema called *The Reindeer Wept*. Never heard of it, have you? Exactly.

Not every member of the department was as gifted or as eager as I was, but only one of them truly resisted the consultant's program. Professor Tryon simply refused to abandon the notion that there was some inherent value in the humanities and that it was our task, our noble task, to inspire students with a love of literature and art, to teach them critical thinking, to make them life-long learners, and blah blah blah. You can imagine how hollow that nonsense sounded to me, who had felt a book turn to nothing under my hand, and who knew that a book could turn to nothing only because it had never been anything. Just a bit of filthy slime draining away, oozing through the cracks.

Even so, I hadn't fully accepted the consultant's teaching into my soul. What held me back was Professor Tryon herself. Our friendship.

My love, held in my heart like a secret pearl. The way she made my daughter laugh. The way her breath felt on my cheek, soft and warm.

The crisis came at the end of the spring semester. The state legislature's cuts were even more drastic than we'd expected. The public education budget was slashed to the bone. Rumors swirled around campus that the administration was going to disband our department, get rid of the humanities altogether.

Professor Tryon was in a frenzy. She sent an email to the entire department, demanding an emergency meeting to discuss how we would resist the coming onslaught. When Professor Casimir demurred, she scheduled the meeting herself. It would take place on a Thursday evening in the seminar room where we usually met, and though it was not on the official department calendar, we all knew that everyone, even Professor Casimir, would attend.

And this is the key room. After you! No, don't bother with the light switch. The lights don't work in here. I'll just use the flashlight on my phone. Be sure to stay close to me; I know the way, but it's easy to get lost or stumble in the dark. Lots of things to trip over, lots of junk lying around. All sorts of trash and garbage. You might want to cover your nose.

But it's nice in here all the same, isn't it? No fluorescents. No infernal humming.

Professor Tryon's meeting was as wild and chaotic as you'd expect. She stood at the head of the long table, shouting and waving her arms, telling us we'd all be a bunch of cowards if we didn't stand up for ourselves.

"Stand up how?" someone shouted back. "What can we do?"

"What the fuck kind of question is that?" she screamed. "What you should be asking is, what can *they* do without *us*? They need us!

This is a goddamn college, and we're the ones who do the goddamn teaching!"

I'd brought my daughter to the meeting, thinking it would be quick and we could catch the latest Pixar movie afterward. Blushing, I bent down to whisper in her ear. "Sorry about Professor Tryon's potty-mouth, sweetie. She's just upset."

My daughter rolled her eyes. "I've heard way worse."

A sudden crash behind me brought me upright. Cold air gusted against my back, eddying through my hair like questing tendrils. I turned to see the consultant in the doorway, his glasses white with fluorescent splendor. His hand was extended in front of him, trembling, ecstatic. Everyone fell silent. The lights' hum was the shriek of a star devouring itself, collapsing into final darkness.

"What do you want?" Professor Tryon said at last.

The consultant smiled. "I want to help you." As he advanced, the assembled faculty parted before him, cringing away from his flickering hand.

"We've had enough of your help," Professor Tryon said. "We're not going to listen to any more of your bullshit. We're going to fight, and we're going to win."

The consultant approached the head of the table. I turned my daughter away from him, squeezed her against me.

"I'm not here to convince you," the consultant said. "If the department decides that my services are no longer required, I'll accept that decision. I'm not exactly hurting for work, you know. I'm not here because I need to be, or even because I want to be. I'm here because you need me. You need help, Professor Tryon. Let me help you."

"Go fuck yourself," Professor Tryon said. "Don't say one more word to me."

The consultant nodded. Without a word, he raised his transfigured hand to his face and removed his glasses.

I was standing behind the consultant, looking over his shoulder at Professor Tryon. I never saw his eyes without the glasses. But I saw what happened to Professor Tryon's face as she stared into those eyes. I saw the fight drain out of her. I saw her eyes' gleam of defiant hope gutter out. I saw her soul die.

The consultant raised his hand again, replaced his glasses. He held the spread palm out toward Professor Tryon, his fingers quivering inches from her face.

"No!" my daughter screamed. While I'd been watching Professor Tryon, she'd turned back toward the consultant, and now she struggled out of my grip and dashed toward him. "Don't you dare touch her!"

Before I could move, before I could open my mouth, the consultant whirled around, and the hand that had been reaching for Professor Tryon's face came down on my daughter's head.

When she dissolved, a quiet fell over the room, so deep I couldn't even hear the hum of the lights. The consultant's hand floated in empty air, motionless as the hand of a statue before it's cut from the marble. Motionless as a stone in the windless light of the world's ultimate sunset.

I looked into the consultant's eyes, calm and placid in their glass cage. I looked over his shoulder at Professor Tryon, her face totally empty, her eyes seeing nothing, seeing everything. I looked at the consultant's hand floating in the emptiness that had been my daughter.

I felt nothing. My heart was an empty tomb, cracked and drained. My education was complete.

I stretched out my hand. The consultant took it. We shook.

"I know things seem hopeless," the consultant said. "I know these cuts go deep, and they make it seem like there's no way for this department to continue its mission. But if you'll just think about what we've talked about over this past year, all the things we've helped each other learn and realize, I think you'll see that if we just knuckle down, and tighten our belts, and do more with less, and remember why we chose this career—it wasn't about the money, no, not about the money, it was about the love, wasn't it, yes, the love, the love, the love ..."

"Yes," I said. Tears spilled from my eyes. "Love."

It seems like we've been in this key room a long time, doesn't it? I bet you're asking yourself how far does this goddamn room go on, how far can we trudge along down here in the dark, threading our way between these heaps of junk, these piles of rotting garbage everywhere? How long can this fucking death march last?

Well, just hold your horses. We're getting close. See that gleam up ahead?

It didn't take long for me and the consultant to convince the rest of the faculty that our plan would work. It's pretty simple, when you think about it. When your resources are cut, you have to look at your expenses. What are the major expenses of a college? Well, administration's a big one. So, you dissolve the administration. But that's just the start. Facilities and services, that's another big one. And who demands those facilities and services? Students, of course. So, you dissolve the students. Next, there's non-administrative staff, counselors and custodians and so on. Dissolve them. And what's left? Faculty. That's a tricky one. After all, it's the faculty who were doing the dissolving. But you know what they say—how do you eat an elephant? One bite at a time.

Most of the faculty were no trouble. Even Professor Casimir ... *especially* Professor Casimir. To tell the truth, I think he was grateful to pass the reins over to me. He'd been department head a long time, and that sort of position will wear anyone down. I'm sure it won't be long before it wears me down, too.

A couple of the adjuncts got a bit feisty. Tried to organize a union, get a little collective action going. But we nipped that in the bud before it could cause any real problems.

Oh, I almost forgot one big expense, something colleges spend a lot of money on. Can you guess? That's right—consultants! But I suppose it's the sign of a good consultant that their clients eventually outgrow the need for them. They're like teachers in that way. No prouder moment for a teacher than when your student outpaces you.

In the end, it was just me and Professor Tryon. I hoped it could stay that way, that the two of us could keep working together forever, doing what we love. But it wasn't meant to be. Maybe the consultant's eyes looked too deep into her, hollowed her out too completely. If there's nothing left, nothing at all, then nothing can drain out. And that's what life is, wouldn't you say? A gradual process of draining out? Draining away, drop by drop?

What are you giving me that look for? Is it something I said?

Oh, I see. You really are an aficionado of the humanities, a true close reader. A little while ago, when I said my heart was an empty tomb, all drained out, you made a note of it. Maybe you thought it was a nice little image, or maybe you thought it was a silly, melodramatic cliché. Anyhow, you filed it away. And then when I said that Professor Tryon was totally drained and hollow, so that she couldn't keep going … implying that, since I'm still here talking to you, I'm *not* totally drained … well, isn't that a bit of a contradiction?

Unless, you're thinking with your clever little analyzing brain, unless I've been *replenished* from time to time … unless I keep filling up that cracked, broken heart of mine, filling it up so that it drains out again, then filling it again, and again ...

And now you understand. I see in your eyes that you understand. But now something else is bothering you. If I'm leading you to your doom, leading you through this darkness and filth to a fate that's surely worse than anything you can imagine, why are you still here? Why aren't you running away, screaming for help? Wouldn't any fate—lost in the dark forever, crushed in a landslide of garbage, eaten by rats and cockroaches—wouldn't any terrible end be better than what awaits you, if you come with me?

Yes, it would.

So, why aren't you running away?

Let me ask about something you may not have noticed, even with your feisty adjunct mind. When was the last time I spoke out loud? Think about it. I believe you'll find it was when we were upstairs, standing at your office door. I said something like, "Try jiggling the knob." Since then, you've been hearing my voice, but I haven't been speaking. I've been in your mind, pulling you along on a leash of words. Draining you out, bit by bit.

The consultant's hand was a fearsome weapon, dazzling and swift, but crude. Swish, pop, disappear. My own hand has developed much subtler techniques. If you think back again to our conversation upstairs, you may recall I gave you a reassuring pat on the shoulder.

We're almost there. See! The lights that glare like bursting stars reflected in the eyes of a dead world! Listen! The hum that raves like a billion flies at feast!

Oh, stop blubbering. What are you losing, really? You're a humanities adjunct, you probably would have frozen to death in your car over winter break.

Here we are. Just look into the light. Just let the hum wash over you. Soon you'll remember why you chose this career, and you'll find it's not so hard to do more with less.

The Chalk
Martyrs

Eric Raglin

A curl of paint hangs off the classroom wall. That redhead kid with braces—Elias? Elliott?—pulls at it gently, as if he could strip the whole room in one go, peel it like an orange. He flashes a shit-eating metallic grin, daring me to give him detention—or maybe just *attention*.

"Unless you want to repaint the room, you better cut that out," I say. "Do I need to move you?"

He releases the paint and whispers something to the girl beside him. They look at me and laugh.

"Alright, move," I say, pointing to an empty desk at the front of the room.

The boy groans, slides his backpack across the floor, and shuffles to his new seat.

Day one at this school and I'm working to build my reputation as the teacher who takes no shit and won't smile until Christmas. The kids will learn to respect me and, god willing, they'll learn to read, too.

That paint is going to be a problem though. Doesn't matter who sits there. Some bored kid whose phone ran out of battery will pick at that curl and make a goddamn mess. I doubt we'll get a fresh coat anytime soon, what with this classroom reeking of budget cuts. The freshman English textbooks have loose binding and not a single story published after 1980. The desks are one "oh captain, my captain" moment away from collapsing. And the whiteboard is Sharpied with a decade of vulgar graffiti that no custodian could scrub off.

This isn't the well-funded Eastwood High I taught at last year. This is a national embarrassment.

The last bell of the day rings, and my students rush out of the room.

"Get a parent signature on that syllabus and bring it back tomorrow," I call after them.

Maybe two students hear me.

When they're gone, I step into the hallway and savor the sound of the school emptying. I glaze over with relief and exhaustion.

"Kel, how'd your first day go?" A cheery voice across the hall. It's Caroline Post, the other sophomore English teacher. She smiles and walks toward me with a slight limp.

I'm about to respond, but I stop dead when I see her classroom through the wide-open door. It's like a portal to another world, or at least another school—one with a budget still in the green. Fresh paint, a top-of-the-line short-throw projector, rows of adjustable standing desks, and a collection of textbooks without so much as a scuff on their spines. Is this a seniority thing?

Caroline catches me staring. "It's nice, isn't it?" she says. "Had to give up a lot, but it was worth it. Anything for the kids, right?"

"Jesus Christ," I say.

She chuckles. "He doesn't get credit this time."

"Who, then? You? On a teacher's salary?" I rub my temples, failing to make sense of the math with my English teacher brain. No way she could afford all that unless she lives at school and sleeps on that couch in the teacher's lounge. Probably not even then.

"You'll learn soon enough," she says with something between a smile and a wince.

A shiver runs down my spine, and I consider exploring why, but the clock says it's time to go home.

"Well, I'll see you tomorrow," I say, closing my classroom door.

"Leaving early?" she asks, and I hate the way she asks it—like she's about to report my answer to Jolene Bennett, our supervising administrator.

"Leaving at contract time," I say.

Work-life boundaries are vital. I learned that the hard way at Eastwood, teaching an extra prep, coaching speech, and grading papers in bed every night until I passed out. For the sake of my sanity, I had to switch schools and get a fresh start.

As I walk away from the English wing, Caroline's eyes tickle the back of my head like lice.

———◆◇◆———

While the kids are circling up for small-group *Macbeth* discussions, a desk implodes into a heap of warped metal and splintered particle board. It's Elliott's, and as much as I'm inclined to blame him—*you jumped on it, didn't you? Trying to make your friends laugh, right?*—his wide-eyed expression tells me he's innocent. The desk was a piece of shit. Its time had come, much like Banquo's.

"Guess I have to share with Aiden," Elliott says, giggling as he wriggles onto his friend's lap.

"Come to daddy," Aiden says, flicking his tongue and then laughing like he single-handedly invented comedy.

I march toward them with a stern finger raised. "Totally inappropriate. And do *not* sit on—"

The second desk breaks. Elliott and Aiden are tangled, cackling in the rubble.

"Out! Out!" I say, my face hot and voice straining. "To the office, *now!*"

Half of the kids are laughing, and a couple are yelling at Aiden for being gross. I picture every object in this room crumbling to dust, joining the ruin. How the hell can I teach like this? How can the kids learn?

Fuck this. I'll talk with Caroline again. Doesn't matter that she gives off creepy cop vibes. I need to know how she got such a nice classroom.

After the chaos and referrals and terrible *Macbeth* discussions ("Mr. D, is Lady Macbeth hot?"), the kids finally leave and I get my chance to talk with Caroline. I poke my head into her classroom. She's helping a girl on some writing assignment, but when she sees me, she whispers, "Work on that paragraph transition. I'll be right back." Limping and smiling, she joins me in the hall.

"Didn't think you'd still be here," she says. "Isn't it nearly contract time?"

She doesn't offer a playful wink. Just that ceaseless smile, which is so much worse.

"Look, about that," I say. "I'm not lazy. I care about the kids. I do. And I want to know how you managed to … you know, give them what they deserve."

Her smile widens even farther, and I swear I hear the corners of her lips stretching, about to tear. A sound like wet, squeaky rubber.

"I'm so glad you asked," she says.

But I'm not sure *I'm* glad. Maybe this is the worst mistake of my life.

"Let me finish with Luisa first," Caroline says. "And then I'll take you down to the old bomb shelter."

"Bomb shelter?" I ask, and something in her tone makes me want to run away.

"That's right. Bomb shelter," she says. "*Boom*."

———◦•◦———

Apparently the school issues every teacher a key to the bomb shelter—as if it's the Cold War all over again—but I haven't received mine yet. In Caroline's excitement to show me what's down there, she forgets hers.

"Oh, shoot," she says, slapping her thigh. But her eyes brighten when she sees a hunchbacked old custodian. "Bill! Thank God you're here. Any chance you could unlock the shelter for us?"

"Of course, darling," Bill says.

The man takes his sweet time finding the key on a ring that must weigh five pounds, and he chats up a storm while he searches. I get the feeling he needs someone to talk to. Lonely job it must be scraping dried gum off desks after most people have left for the day.

"My grandson, Parker," Bill says, leisurely flipping through the keys, "he got himself a baseball scholarship. Would you believe that? Wish I could've gone to college on a baseball scholarship. Oh well, you live and you learn and you mop floors for forty years."

He unleashes a laugh halfway between joy and agony, and I'm unsure whether to join him or cringe. Caroline closes her eyes, softens her smile, and nods.

"It's never too late, Bill," she says. "All of us are lifelong learners."

"And some of us are bone tired," Bill replies, laughing again, but it's more of a wheeze this time. "Ah, here we go."

He pinches a scratched, discolored key and unlocks the door. The crumbled concrete stairs leading down are too narrow, designed for a time when this school housed half the students it does now. Musty black mold rises to greet us. My nose wrinkles, but Bill stares down the passage, seemingly untroubled, impervious after decades spent battling filth.

"Still want to know, Kel?" Caroline asks.

The question is a test—one I plan to pass. I don't answer with words, for fear that I'll cough and look weak. Instead, I take the lead, marching down the ruin of stairs and hoping I don't fall on my face. Caroline makes a pleased humming sound and follows.

"Holler when you're done and I'll lock up," Bill says. There's a sadness in his voice as if Caroline and I are friends abandoning him for our own little adventure. Poor guy.

"Left at the end of the staircase," Caroline says.

I reach the bottom and turn. Dim orange bulbs light the corridor, flickering like dying fireflies. In front of me is a massive dirt-floored room. Shelves line the sides, filled with rusted cans of food and dusty water jugs. This bomb shelter is a relic, untouched and poorly preserved. With a little care, this place could be a museum, a hands-on learning opportunity for the History students.

"Watch out for the chasm," Caroline says, and I'm jolted back to reality.

That's when I see it, running through the center of the room: a huge gash in the dirt that plunges to God knows where. I imagine its jaws widening and devouring the school.

"Ready to know the truth?" Caroline asks.

"Sure," I say, but I have no idea where this is going. "What am I looking at here?"

"Come."

She walks toward the chasm and sits at its edge, too close for comfort. My palms are sweating, but I join her, giving myself an extra foot of space. The dirt feels damp and cold against my ass.

"So, uh, what's the deal then?" I ask. "I don't get it."

Caroline lifts her left foot and works to remove her glossy, creme-colored wedge. I peek over the edge, hoping there's water in the chasm, a hot spring bubbling to the surface to relax our feet at the end of the day. Of course, it's a stupid wishful thought. The chasm is dark all the way down, and how far that is, I have no way of knowing.

A *pop* catches my attention—Caroline pulling off her shoe.

"What are—?"

Her pinky toe is missing. No, not just missing. *Cleaved*. Stuck to the exposed meat is a cotton ball, pink and red and yellow with drainage.

The sour sludge of a half-digested protein bar rises in my throat.

"Kel, don't run," Caroline says. "I'm okay, really. And the students are more than okay. You saw what they have now."

"This is sick," I say. "Why are you doing this?"

"For the kids, of course. All they need is a little help from, well ..."

She nods toward the chasm. Its darkness seems to spill over, stretching toward my own toes. I scoot back. The illusion evaporates.

"Kel," Caroline says. "I gave one small thing to them, and they gave the children everything."

"Them?" I ask, but I don't want to know. Never have I wanted an answer less.

Another woman's voice down the corridor: "Caroline, is that you? And Kel?"

I whip around, wide-eyed as a scared puppy, and there's admin Jolene, silhouetted in the dim light. She pulls down her glasses and gets a good look at us. I swear we're about to get reprimanded for whatever sick shit this is, but no. She smiles.

"Thanks for showing Kel the ropes, Caroline," she says. "Another Chalk Martyr will do us good, especially after the Miss Robbins incident. Kel, I'll put a key in your mailbox so you can come down here whenever you're—"

"Excuse me," I say, and that protein bar is coming up.

Puke reaches my tongue and I'm running away from Caroline and past Jolene, stumbling up those unstable stairs. I pass Bill on my way out, and he gives me a *howdy*, but I don't have time to respond. Getting the hell out is the only thing that matters.

———◦———

Caroline isn't the only one who's given part of herself to *them*—whoever the hell *they* are. I don't have hard proof, but I teach my students to make educated guesses based on available information, and I'm damn good at making those myself. The evidence is there every time I step into the teachers lounge.

Just like Caroline, Brit Hubbard, one of the Art teachers, walks with a limp. She looks too young to have one—young enough to be mistaken for one of the students—and I'm sure if she took her heels off, one of her piggies would already be off to market.

Then there's the Gym teacher Mae Foltz with her missing ear. The scar tissue is red, inflamed, and ugly—more DIY than surgical. Why she chose to remove such a visible part of her body is a mystery to me, but maybe that's the point: to display her sacrifice proudly. A medal of ruined cartilage.

The worst is Al Sands, the History teacher with an eye patch. I can only hope it's a prop for some lesson he's giving about the Age of Sail, but my gut tells me there's a sunken pit behind that black fabric. Whether he extracted the eye himself or with another teacher's help, I'd rather not know.

In the lounge, I stand by the microwave, waiting for last night's enchiladas to heat up. The mutilated teachers stare at me from across the room, eating their cashews and sipping their Cokes and waiting for me to join their ranks. Caroline probably told them all about me running out on her.

But I'm glad I did. I don't need to martyr myself for these kids. They can sit in their collapsing desks, reading textbooks printed before the collapse of the Soviet Union, and they can peel paint off the wall when they zone out during lectures.

That fucking paint.

Nope, there are some things I can't ignore. Maybe these teachers are right. We can't teach like this, and the kids can't learn. But there has to be a bloodless solution. I swear to God, I'll find it.

———•◦•———

Every class copy of *Fahrenheit 451* has pages missing. Elliott asks if someone ripped them out and burned them. I know he's being a shit, but it means he's paying attention to the book—or what's left of it. I feel proud.

When one student reaches a missing page, another student loans their copy with that section intact. This is how we operate until we reach pages 243 to 244. We're nearly at the end, but somehow, those pages are missing from every single copy. Even my teacher's edition.

"Can't we just Sparknotes it?" Aiden groans.

"*Spark* notes," Elliott says. "Get it? Like burning a book?"

And how did Elliott, of all students, become this kid? I never saw it coming.

"Shut the hell up, dude," Aiden says, then slams his open book facedown, cracking its already-ailing spine.

"Absolutely none of that," I say. "Aiden, what did we talk about before?"

"Yeah, yeah," he says. "Sorry."

He lays his head on his desk. When I look around the room, he isn't the only one with his head down. These students are exhausted, defeated, sick of piecing together a book from 25 fragmented copies. How can anyone—except Elliott, evidently—learn like this?

I think back to the bomb shelter, to the chasm. To *them*. I'm not ready to give myself up, but their call is growing stronger.

———•O•———

Opportunity strikes, sudden and terrible.

It's that one-in-a-million night where I'm somehow the last teacher in the building. Putting off a month's worth of grading until the day before parent-teacher conferences will do that.

The last thing I want after reading a hundred shitty *Of Mice and Men* papers and only a half dozen decent ones is to talk to anyone, but just my luck, there's Bill the custodian between me and the school exit. I could take the long way and go out a different door, but it'd be obvious. Don't want to hurt the guy's feelings.

"Kel!" he says, grinning. Without looking down, he folds a cafeteria table in half and pushes it against the wall. Forty years in this job and he could do it blindfolded. "Listen, did I tell you my grandson got noticed by some Minor League coach? I know it's not Major, but heck, you gotta start somewhere."

"Well, tell your grandson congrats," I say, zipping my jacket and inching toward the exit. No guarantee Bill will take the hint; guys this lonely generally don't, or they choose not to.

"Yeah, I'm darn proud of the boy," he says, moving to the next table, still not looking down. "I like to give myself a little credit, what with all the catch we played when he was—"

The second he folds the cafeteria table, he stops. At first, I think he's just done talking, and a wave of relief passes over me, but then I see his face go white and his hand go red. The man gasps and clutches his wound. His pinky finger is gone—snapped off in the table's jaws—and the stump of flesh gushes all over the sleeve of his blue button-up.

"Cocksucking motherfucker!" he screams.

Howling, he kicks the floor like an enraged bull and, without realizing it, sends his missing finger flying. The digit skitters and lands beneath a wheeled garbage bin.

I'm frozen for only a moment before I realize what's happened and what I have to do. I whip out my phone, dial 911, tell them the man in front of me is bleeding the fuck out. I don't know if that's true, but from the way Bill is moaning, he needs a medic fast. I hang up, rip off my jacket, and tell him to clamp it over the wound. He does so, whimpering. Flecks of spit collect at the corners of his mouth.

And the plan is already coming to me. A plan that is every kind of awful.

"Where'd the finger go, Bill?" I ask, playing dumb. The question catches in my throat, and God, I hate lying like this. "Did you see where it landed?"

Wide-eyed and pale, Bill scans the floor, looking like he might tip over at any moment.

"I—I don't—I don't see—" he starts, and I rush over to steady him.

"Don't worry about it," I say. "We'll find it. Just keep clamping down on the wound until they arrive. I'll do some searching, okay?"

He nods in a way that tells me his pain has overridden his capacity to understand words. I grab him a plastic cafeteria chair, and he plops down into it.

Sirens outside. Help will be here any moment. I know what I have to do.

I eye the wheeled garbage bin. It's an okay hiding spot, but the medics will still be able to find the finger there.

There's a vent beside the bin. I check on Bill. His head is lulling and his eyes are squinted in agony. He's not looking at me. I run for the bin and dive like I'm a baseball star sliding into home plate.

Baseball. He'll still be able to play catch with three fingers and a thumb, right?

There it is, among the fallen french fries and lost pencils: Bill's pinky.

The medics are pounding on the exit door. They don't have a key, and I'm supposed to let them in. If I were a good man, I'd greet them with the missing finger in hand. But tonight I'm not a good man; I'm a good teacher. One who goes above and beyond for his students.

I slip the pinky through the vent grate. The medics won't find it there. After they've given up and left, it will be mine.

———◦———

I normally pull into the parking lot fifteen minutes before school starts, but today I arrive at the crack of dawn. Caroline drives up a few seconds after me—first and last time that'll happen—and I can't wait to talk. I'm smiling and sweating and standing right outside her driver's side door. I probably look like I've got the hots for her, but no, I'm just excited to share that I've joined the Chalk Martyrs, to witness how my classroom has transformed overnight.

She opens her car door and stands, wincing at the pressure on her mutilated foot. When she sees me grinning, she smirks. "You joined the club, didn't you?"

I stride toward her with newfound confidence.

"The cult, more like it," I say, and my neck burns. Why did I say that? Cults do fucked up shit. *I* did fucked up shit. I can't dwell on what's already done. "Anyway, yeah, I'm pumped to see what—"

Caroline looks me up and down as if she's a factory worker doing a quality control inspection. I know what she's searching for, what she's going to ask. But shit, she'll never believe the story I'd prepared about cutting off my big toe. Not when I just swaggered up to her, limp free and cocky. I need to come up with something else, and quick.

"You only need one kidney, right?" I say. My mouth goes dry. I've overplayed my hand, haven't I? If I ripped out my own kidney last night, I wouldn't be here this morning. Or no, maybe I would. Because I'm a *good* teacher. A *committed* teacher. One who works through the pain to serve the kids. I straighten my back and feign a wince—gotta sell the story.

Caroline's eyes go wide. When the initial shock fades, she claps her hands over mine and squeezes. "It's been so long since we last had a teacher like you," she says. "I'll admit, I didn't think you had the drive, but I'm happy to be proven wrong." She smiles, shakes her head, and chuckles. "Let's go see what they brought you."

———◦—

My classroom is empty. Everything gone, save for the dust bunnies and gray disks of gum dried to the floor and that fucking curl of paint hanging off the wall. The dust and gum would be gone too if Bill had been here to clean last night, but of course his shift came to a sudden end.

Bill … fuck.

I feel like crying or fleeing or putting a gun in my mouth. I feel like cutting off my own finger and going to the hospital and donating it to Bill—a digit not yet wracked with arthritic pain.

"Liar," Caroline says.

I jump, half because I'd forgotten she was here and half because her voice is low and seething and full of bad omens.

"I don't know what you did," she continues, "but you never—and I mean *never*—piss them off. This is Miss Robbins all over again."

"What?" I ask, even though I heard her right the first time. My question comes out all nasal, like I'm about to sob. And here they come, the ugly, choking tears.

"Leave—*now*," Caroline says. "If you want to live."

I obey and run down the hallway toward the exit. Maybe it's my imagination, but I feel their eyes on me, glaring through the gaps in ventilation grates and lockers, plotting my death. Something skitters across the marble floor behind me, and as much as I want to know what they look like, I don't dare turn around.

When I reach the parking lot, I'm panting and my throat tastes like blood. It's no safer out here. My prickling neck still senses them, lurking atop the roof and behind the staff bike rack. They'll follow me wherever I run. I wonder if Miss Robbins, whoever she was, tried to escape this same way.

I get to my car and scramble for the key. Other teachers are pulling up, and maybe they think I forgot something at home—my lunch or my laptop or a fat stack of graded papers.

But I can already tell they know the truth. They know I've never been a Chalk Martyr and never will be. That I've never known sacrifice and my students have never gotten the education they deserve.

The true Chalk Martyrs know I'm being hunted, and they are glad for it.

Jumping into my car, I screech out of the parking lot and don't look back. This is it. My teaching days are over. Everything is over.

Make Sure You Fill out Those Evaluations

Aurelius Raines II

H ello.

My name is Robert Darnell, uh, I'll be your facilitator this afternoon.

Now, before we get started, I just wanted to make sure that the doors have been secured. I know teacher inservice professional development can be "off" because of the changes in schedule. So I just want to make sure the doors are secured before we go any further.

So could someone—Oh … okay. You got it? Thanks.

The last thing we want is any interruptions during our professional development.

Okay, we got a lot to cover, so let's get right to it.

As I said, my name is Rob and I have been a teacher for eighteen years. That's right. I was teaching before the dead walked the earth, back when all pandemics required was a mask and some hand sanitizer. Haha!

Yeah. So, I was actually at work when the outbreak really got bad. The school where I worked was "okay" on security, but some of the staff had already come into the building with infections because they were out of sick days.

Yeah. Right?

I know. But it was a different time.

Anyway, by the time we were done with Reading, there were about twenty dead in the hallway. They were scratching at the door because they were attracted by the phonics chant we'd been doing.

Yeah. I know. Like I said, different time.

Long-short, I got the kids out safely and to an evacuation zone, and since then I've been an advocate for student safety in the time of the Zombie Pandemic.

Now, show of hands, who also started teaching before the pandemic? Not a lot of you ... oh, okay ... I see one. Good. When did you start? ... Wow ... Nice. So you've been at this for a while ... really ... you had to take a leave of absence. Why? Well ... I can probably guess ... Oh, your arm! How did you lose it? ... third-grader? No? Oh ... three-year-old? Yeesh. Yeah. Those teeth are sharp even when they're *not* the flesh-eating ghouls. Well, I applaud you. You have been out here doing the work. I salute you, ma'am. I look forward to any insight you can provide to my presentation.

Alright, you should already have a packet in front of you. Feel free to take notes. I also have the presentation in a pdf that's been sent to your email.

The internet is down? Well, hopefully it'll be back up. I know your principal has already downloaded a copy. She can send it to you later.

Let's get started.

Since the first cases of the zombie virus were discovered in London, ten years ago, it has been estimated that some 500 million people have been infected with the Pandoravirus lemminkainen or the "zombie virus." So what does this mean?

Wait ... Oops ...

One slide too far.

Here we go ...

This means that we are losing skilled labor at epidemic rates and it's up to us to provide a safe environment for tomorrow's workers. So today we are going to talk about safety through 3 modalities.

Building security, (*now* it's time for this slide), Self-defense—yeah ... I know. Trust me. We'll get through it—and of course, First Aid.

Now, I noticed that this is a pretty secure building. But I also notice that there are a lot of glass walls in the building lobby. You did the smart thing and put cages over the windows, but you can still see through into the building. Now, while I understand this feels safe enough, in reality, the kids are still really visible. Remember: Fresh zombies still have fairly good vision. With those open windows, arrival and dismissal will look like a buffet for any passing zombie. And you know what they say: One curious zombie makes a thousand curious zombies. Correct me if I'm wrong, but I'm sure you all have already had a few pileups by those windows.

What ... really? ... last week? Well, there you go. You have a pileup of zombies outside the school, now you have to do compartmentalization and fortification protocols, and even if it doesn't get to that point, the moaning and the banging is a distraction to instruction. You can't think, the kids can't think ...

So, let's talk about window blinds or even heavy-duty curtains. They don't have to be the security type ... just something that reduces the sound conducted through the glass and, of course, hides the fact that there are actually living people inside the building. And if your "blinding discipline" is tight, then you can go a whole day without even knowing there is a pandemic going on.

Yeah ... right? ... I know. I *wish!*

Now, I notice that you all have a covered and secured carport from the drop off point to the school.

Is there somebody checking for fever and bites at the door?

Good.

My first time seeing a zombie in a school building, it pretty much walked in off the street. Now, in the school's defense, this was one of the first days of the outbreak. I don't even think they were even saying "zombie" at this point. It was a parent, in fact, dropped their kid off, turned, and then shambled right back into the building.

Haha ... yeah ... I know. Still not as bad as an impromptu parent conference, right?

Anyhow ... yeah. Parent must have infected a few. By the time I knew what was going on ... well. You can imagine ...

Now, I noticed that when I came in here, today, I wasn't tested with VLA. Do you normally ... No? What is a VLA? Are you kid—

Sorry.

Yes. The CDC made Viral Load Analyzers part of the mitigation guidelines for all public buildings last year.

I'm surprised y—

Oh ... okay. Well there you have it. The VLAs are on back order and this school could not get them.

In the meantime, you know what to look for: pale, cold, and clammy skin. Unusual marks, wounds, or bites. Dramatically low body temp. Anything below 95 degrees should be monitored.

Now, do you have an isolation room to keep any kids that are possibly infected?

Heh?

Kinda?

Well. Okay. What's "kinda?" Really ... okay ... well ... okay. Geeze. You definitely wanna get that fixed.

Because ... yeah ... like ... what if the kid chews through the rope. You don't even have a chain? And what happens if someone needs to go to the equipment cage to get gym equipment?

Oh. You don't have any. They cut PE? Well ... that solves *that* problem. Haha. Yeah ... hehe.

So ... yeah. Um. (Geeze).

Well, like I said. Let's move on to the next section.

Self-defense.

Now, should there be a breach and zombies actually get into the school, you will need to clear the building. Do you have a security team? I didn't see any at the ...

Oh, you do. Do they guard the door?

Wait ... That guy? He's ... he's ... probably seen a lot of action. Is it just him or is there someone ... younger? I mean, there's nothing wrong with experience. Lots of experience. But do you think he'll be up to ... well.

Okay.

Moving on.

You should have a plan with security to organize, isolate, and shelter.

Good question. Why isolate? So, until recently, we followed conventional shelter-in-place protocols. A holdover from the live shooter emergency protocols from twenty years ago.

But ... well, think about it. A zombie gets into the school and you got thirty or forty kids huddled together in one room. And one of them is already infected. They turn in the room while everyone is locked inside and you're gonna open the door to the whole school being overrun with its own students and staff.

Right, makes sense?

So, there was an idea borrowed from nautical design. Ships are designed so that if a section takes on water, the bulkheads close that part of the ship off so the water doesn't fill the craft.

Same idea here. The students are broken up into smaller groups. This way, if infection breaks out in one group, then the spread is limited to the small group. It's dark but that's the reality that we live in now.

Questions?

Yes?

Well, as with all of our other protocols, staff should check the hallways and nearby bathrooms for "stragglers." Make sure they are not infected and then let them isolate until the security team ... I mean ... guy ... gives the all clear.

So, ummm. This is not in the slide show. But I wanted to talk about the new legislation that is coming concerning firearms in the classroom. Should there be a breach, then having a firearm on hand might be the difference between life and death for your students. I think the current legislation, as it's proposed, would mean a handgun and a bladed weapon for each room. Of course, you should be ready for what this will mean for you and your school. Unfortunately, it looks like a few conservative members of the House are holding up the bill to fund firearms in "urban schools" because they are scared that the guns will be used in crimes rather than in an emergency.

Yeah ... I know. I can't ...

Well ...

Suffice it to say, whatever legislation is passed, we need to be re-sourceful when it comes to defending our students. So guns or not, we need to be thinking resourcefully about what is already on campus and how it can be used for self-defense.

Now, I don't have to tell you how to best neutralize the undead. I'm sure most of you probably learned how to kill a zombie in your education courses. We can—that's right, destroy the brain.

So here's what we're going to do. I want you to use the large memo pad that is already stuck to your table and work with everyone in your group to brainstorm some items you have around here that can possibly be used as a weapon against zombies. You got five minutes.

Are you ready?

Go!

———————

Okay, That's time. Let's see what you've got.

Group 1?

Okay. Interesting list. Well. By interesting, I mean short.

Haha.

You just said pencils and pens. And I'm sure you might have some other resources.

Funny story.

The first day of the outbreak, I actually protected a room full of preschoolers with a large writing pencil. Up until then, I'd always thought those pencils were big enough to stake a vampire. (Knock on wood). Haha!

Let's hear from the other groups.

Group 2?

... I see ... you don't have much different than Group 1. It was pretty sharp to consider disassembling the desks. But if you can do that, then you have a screwdriver, right? No? ... right ... hex wrenches. Haha ...

how did I forget? Yeah ... but still ... good luck with taking the legs off those desks with those little wrenches in an emergency.

C'mon. I wanna hear some other ideas.

Group 3? Impress me.

Oh ... I see ... You got the same things.

Well. Huh. That's interesting. Bladed yardstick. Okay ... how would that work, exactly? Do you have one? Yeah ... that may be hard to engineer for a few reasons.

So ...

Have you all considered your sports teams? The bats, right? Natural clubs ... right th—

Oh ... really.

So you're saying you have *none* on campus. Not-a-one? How?

They cut all of them? Even chess? So, not field hockey sticks? Well, those are pretty much useless anyway. Do you have a weight room? No ... right ... a grammar school.

So, no bats on campus, at all. Anything dangerous?

No?

No.

Okay. Well. It's important to make the school a safe place for students. Even if that means you don't have anything to protect the stu—

Okay. I'm getting the "keep it moving" sign from the principal.

I mean ... Has anyone, at the least, brought anything from home?

Right. Maybe that's a discussion for another time. Like ... when the principal isn't in the room.

Haha.

Okaaaay. Moving on.

Why don't we take a break for lunch and we'll talk about first aid when we come back. Okay. See ya.

Hey. Anyone know if that burger place is still open over here? They had the best fri--

Oh.

Overrun?

Wow ... okay. That's too bad. I was looking forward to those fries.

Okay.

Welcome back.

Okay. Let's—let's get ... If I can get you all to quiet down—

Clap once if you can hear me.

Clap twice if you can hear me.

Thanks. Welcome back.

So, before the break we talked about securing the school, making sure the kids stay safe inside and the zombies are *not* safe inside. Over lunch, I made note of some of the changes you may want to make around the school based on your feedback. I've also sent out an evaluation I would like you to fill out before we leave today. It's just your thoughts on how you feel about this training ... me ... these shoes. (Chuckle)

Okay, enough fooling around.

So ...

Sorry ... getting the slide back up here.

Good. Here we go.

Like I was saying, we talked about protecting the school and keeping zombies out. But what about if all else fails and a kid gets infected. Show of hands. Who has had a student show up to school infected?

Wow.

Wow. That's a lot. Th—

I'm …

(silence)

Yeah … Yeah. I know. I'm sorry. It's okay. That's really sad. Here's some tissue. Do you wanna step out?

Okay.

Yeah.

So … Boy. That's a really heavy thing right? These are little kids who are under our care, yet, no matter how we do things right *inside* the building, we really can't control what happens *outside* the building. And despite our best efforts, one of the kiddos comes in with a cough in Phonics and a full-on desire for human flesh by Math. So, what do you do?

I imagine that you all actually have a process for contact tracing, right? I'm sure you use the standard ZCease program or—

Murray? You're still using Murray?

Oh … Boy. So, like, how do you account for all the vectors? How do you have time to talk to all the students to figure out who came in contact before it has time to spread?

What's ZCease? I'll send your principal some information, but basically, each kid is tracked by a wristband when they come into the building. If one of them is discovered to be infected, then you can just access an app that spits out a list of other students who have been in contact with the infected and should be isolated. It's pretty cool. Yeah.

Oh … wow … t—this is the form you use. Paper, huh?

Well, you may want to look into ZCease. No. *Z-* Cease. Sure, *Z-C-E-A-S-E*. Yeah. Just look into it and see. Much safer and it'll save you all a lot more time.

So. Where was I?

Okay. We can skip this slide then. Yeah, "ZCease Tips and Tricks" don't apply here, I guess.

Okay. Yep. Here we go.

Okay. Let's talk about the worst case scenario. Kid comes to school and they are infected. How do you stop the school from being compromised and maybe even overrun? We all know what a distraction an outbreak can be. A fifth-grader turns and the whole day is thrown into shambles, right? (See what I did there?) ... haha!

Lesson plans out the window, forms, parent calls, locked down in isolation all day.

So, let's talk about some ways we can make sure that this doesn't become too big of an issue and we minimize the damage.

So here, on the next few slides, you see the first three rules of infection mitigation.

Rule 1) Isolation

Rule 2) Isolation

Rule 3) Isolation

And we can't stress that enough. After a kiddo looks like they might be coming down with the chompers, the only other person they should see is the school nurse.

Oh ...

No nurse.

Oh. Well. Then they should stay in isolation. Now, I've been to schools where the isolation rooms are really just one big room. This is a mistake when we consider that early stages of infection just look like a bad flu. So, the last thing you want to do is have a relatively healthy kid locked in with a kid who got the chompers and now you got a problem on your hands.

We talked earlier that you have an isolation room. It was the old sports supply room, right?

Is it segmented to keep the kids separated?

That's coming?

This summer? Do we have a plan to keep multiple kids separated in the meantime?

Working on it?

Okay. Working on it.

Well. That's it.

Again. (Sigh) ...

I can't tell you how catastrophic it can be if too many kids are together and one of them is infected. It just takes one bite and you're the next news story.

Now, I know this is controversial in some school districts. But vaccines. Making sure students have access to in-school vaccines will at best prevent students from turning and, at worst, provide you with some time bef—

Aaaannnnd I'm getting the principal shaking their head.

No?

No vaccines in school.

Are they, at least, mandatory before enrollment?

Not here.

(Sigh)

Yeah, I know. I know there is a lot of push back. But the rest of the kids—

I see.

Well.

Next slide.

Finally, First Aid.

I want you to get into groups and we'll discuss treating bites and, if necessary, emergency amputation.

Everyone should have a kit, a practice dummy, and a checklist.

Now. Has anyone been through this training before?

Good, I see a few of you have. Please feel free to help out the first-timers.

———◦———

Alright! That should be our last round of practice. You all will get a certificate of completion. I know that was a hard one, right? Just remember it's always preferable to send home a partial kid than a shambling one. Yeah. Dark but true.

While you all clean up the practice dummies, let's wrap things up.

We're all together? Good. I'm almost done here.

Last slide. I promise.

Just because the undead are walking the Earth, it doesn't mean that students can't receive a quality education. The challenges that our world is facing are legion. Literally. Legions of the undead. And we only have two responsibilities. First, to keep them safe and, second, to educate them. It's easy to forget that's what we're here for. There are some that say if our kids just need to know how to kill the undead and dispose of the bodies, then we've done our jobs.

And I guess an argument can be made for that. I guess we can aim for that low bar. But I started teaching in a time when we still had our sights set on planets and stars. A time when we wanted to explore the oceans. When a brain-controlling virus wasn't our primary medical concern. A time when we survived for a little more than just keeping the economy moving under the worst conditions. I became a teacher in a time when we saw our children as more than an expendable resource "but the [children] of life's longing for itself," to paraphrase Gibran. Now I hate to sound like a sentimental old man ... but I like to think that we can still make our schools and classrooms what we used to call "safe spaces." Places where we could hold the concerns of the outside world at bay long enough to give children time to dream. It is our ... respons—

What?

Oh.

Oh, no!

Okay ... the building has been breached. Did we check the doors after lunch?

Great! Just great!

(Sigh.) Okay.

Looks like we're about to put some of what we learned into practice. I only have one glock and a few magazines, but I bought a few of those demonstration machetes. If someone could help me pass those out. If your classroom or office is nearby and you have those "emergency school supplies," now's the time.

Okay, folks. Remember: downward strokes. Let gravity do some of the work. An exhausted teacher is an infected teacher.

Oh.

And don't forget to fill out those evaluations.

Now, let's go be great educators!

Author Bios

Corey Farrenkopf lives on Cape Cod with his wife, Gabrielle, and works as a librarian. His work has been published in *Uncharted*, *Three-Lobed Burning Eye*, *Smokelong Quarterly*, *Reckoning*, *Bourbon Penn*, *Tiny Nightmares*, *Flash Fiction Online*, *The Dread Machine*, and elsewhere. To learn more, follow him on twitter @CoreyFarrenkopf or on the web at CoreyFarrenkopf.com

Cynthia Gómez (she/her) is a writer and researcher. She writes horror and other types of speculative fiction, set primarily in Oakland, where she makes her home. She has a particular love for themes of revenge, retribution, and resistance to oppression. She has stories in *Fantasy Magazine*, *The Acentos Review*, and *Strange Horizons*, as well as the collections *Antifa Splatterpunk* and *Bag of Bones: 206-Word Stories*. Her novelette, "The Shivering World," was published in Volume Two of the *Split Scream* novelette series. You can find her on Twitter at @cynthiasaysboo. She loves to write dark and frightening things while cuddling with her shadow, aka her adorable little dog.

Emma E. Murray taught first grade for years before becoming a horror and dark speculative fiction writer. Her stories have appeared in anthologies like *What One Wouldn't Do*, *Obsolescence*, and *Ooze: Little Bursts of Body Horror*, as well as magazines such as *Pyre* and *If There's Anyone Left*. To read more, you can visit her website EmmaE Murray.com or follow her on Twitter @EMurrayAuthor.

Christi Nogle is the author of the Bram Stoker Award® nominated novel *Beulah* (Cemetery Gates Media, 2022) and co-editor with Willow Dawn Becker of the Bram Stoker Award® nominated anthology *Mother: Tales of Love and Terror* (Weird Little Worlds, 2022). Christi's debut short story collection *The Best of Our Past, the Worst of Our Future* is out now from Flame Tree Press. Her collections *Promise* and *One Eye Opened in That Other Place* are coming from Flame Tree Press in 2023 and 2024. Her short stories have appeared in many publications, including *PseudoPod*, *Vastarien*, *Mooncalves*, and *Horror Library*. Follow her at http://christinogle.com and on Twitter @christinogle.

Eric Raglin (he/him) is a Nebraskan horror/Weird fiction writer and the editor for Cursed Morsels Press. His debut short story collection is *Nightmare Yearnings* and his second collection *Extinction Hymns* was published by Brigids Gate Press. Find him at ericraglin.com or on Twitter @ericraglin1992.

Aurelius Raines II writes and lives in Chicago. His short stories and essays have been included in the *Fantasy & Science Fiction*, *Apex Magazine*, *Apparition Literature*, *Fiyah Magazine* and *Luminescent Threads: Connections to Octavia Butler*, which was the winner of the Locus Award in Non-Fiction. He is a Voodoonauts Fellow (c/o '21). In his spare time, he teaches Physics to high-schoolers by showing them how to use science to survive the end of civilization.

D. Matthew Urban hails from Texas and lives in Queens, New York, where he reads weird books, watches weird movies, and writes weird fiction. His stories have appeared or are forthcoming in *Ooze: Little Bursts of Body Horror, Shredded: A Sports and Fitness Body Horror Anthology,* and *Dark Matter Presents: Monster Lairs,* among other venues. He can be found on Twitter @breathinghead.

Content Warnings

There's a Reason They Collect the Pencils: child abuse, references to suicide

Drip Drop: child death, implied abuse

The Teachers' Association: references to child death, gun violence

Auxiliary, Supplementary, Inessential: blood and gore, explcitation

The Consultant's Hand: child death

The Chalk Martyrs: self-harm, mutilation

Make Sure You Fill out Those Evaluations: child death, amputation

Other Cursed Morsels Releases

Shredded: A Sports and Fitness Body Horror Anthology

Reader beware! This sports and fitness body horror anthology is dangerous. Side effects include monstrous steroid transformation, concussion-induced madness, possession by jock ghost, death by yoga cult, and more. Read with caution!

Featuring seventeen reps of terror by Nikki R. Leigh, Tim Meyer, Brandon Applegate, Red Lagoe, Caias Ward, RW DeFaoite, Mae Murray, D. Matthew Urban, Charles Austin Muir, Joe Koch, Michael Tichy, Rien Gray, Robbie Burkhart, Eric Raglin, Matthew Pritt, Madeleine Sardina, Alexis DuBon, and J.A.W. McCarthy.

Antifa Splatterpunk

Fascism didn't die in 1945. Its grave was only temporary. Rising again, this undead ideology shambles into the present, gathering power and spreading destruction wherever it goes.

This monster stalks the pages of *Antifa Splatterpunk*, in which sixteen horror writers explore fascism's many terrors: police wielding strange bioweapons against the public, white supremacists annihilating their enemies through dark magic, and TV personalities vilifying all who defy the rising fascist tide.

But these stories are resistance: Nazi-killing demons, Confederate-slaying witches, and everyday people punching fascists in the teeth. Among the gore is a glimmer of hope that one day this monster will return to its grave and never rise again.